(

THE FINAL
FALCON
SAYS I DO

THE FINAL FALCON SAYS I DO

BY

LUCY GORDON

First published in Great Britain 2014
by Mills & Boon, an imprint of Harlequin (UK) Limited,
Large Print edition 2014
Eton House, 18-24 Paradise Road,
Richmond, Surrey, TW9 1SR

ISBN: 978 0 263 24058 0

Harlequin (UK) Limited's policy is to use papers that are natural, renewable and recyclable products and made from wood grown in sustainable forests. The logging and manufacturing processes conform to the legal environmental regulations of the country of origin.

Printed and bound in Great Britain
by CPI Antony Rowe, Chippenham, Wiltshire

To Horus, the Falcon God,
whose magical powers are always there,
lurking mysteriously.

To those the rules [...]
share their thoughts [...]
useful [...]

CHAPTER ONE

IT WOULD BE the wedding of the year. In an elegant, luxurious church in the heart of London, crowded with wealthy, glamorous people, Amos Falcon, the financial giant whose name inspired awe and fury in equal measure, was to escort his stepdaughter down the aisle to be the bride of Dan Connor, a man of wealth and importance in the television industry.

Not that that would impress Amos Falcon. It was common knowledge that he had wanted to marry his stepdaughter to one of his own sons but had failed: one of the few times in his life when he hadn't got his own way.

The excitement level was rising. The wedding wasn't until midday, but the television cameras had been in place an hour earlier. Gossip said the entire Falcon family would be present, which meant Amos's five sons, who hailed from England, America, Russia and France. Some were famous. Some were wealthy. All were notable. And nobody wanted to miss so many fascinating arrivals.

'Travis Falcon,' sighed one young female journalist. 'Oh, I do hope he turns up. I always watch his television series and I'd love to meet him.'

'You reckon he'll really come all the way to London from Los Angeles?' queried Ken, the cameraman with her.

'Why not? He went to Moscow last month for Leonid's wedding. Hey, who's that?'

A buzz of anticipation greeted the arrival of a luxurious car, which disgorged an expensively dressed couple. But then there was a faint groan of disappointment. This man wasn't Travis.

'Marcel Falcon,' Ken mused. 'The French brother. And the one in the car just behind is Leonid.'

He focussed his camera on the two brothers as they climbed the steps to the great entrance and disappeared inside, then switched quickly back to another car from which a man and woman had emerged.

'Darius,' he said. 'English.'

'What about Jackson?' she asked. 'Surely he's

English as well, and after Travis he's the best known because of those TV documentaries he does.'

'He's not a guest. He's the best man and he'll arrive with the groom. After that it'll be Amos and Freya, the bride. Ah, look who's getting out of that car! Freya's mother, the present Mrs Amos Falcon.'

Mrs Falcon was in her fifties, trim, well-dressed, but with an air of quiet reserve that made her stand out in this exotic atmosphere. She hurried up the steps, as though the spotlight made her uneasy.

Just inside the church Darius, Marcel and their wives were waiting for her. They embraced her warmly, and Darius said, 'This must be a happy day for you, Janine. Freya has finally escaped the terrible fate of being married to one of us.'

His stepmother regarded him with wry affection.

'You know very well that I'm fond of you all,' she said, 'and if Freya had really wanted to marry one of you I'd have had no problem. It was the just the way Amos— Well, you know...'

They nodded, understanding her reluctance to

be candid about Amos's determination to get his own way. It had come close to bullying, but a loyal wife couldn't say so.

'How did you persuade him to give her away?' Harriet, Darius' wife, murmured. 'I should think it was the last thing he wanted to do.'

'It was,' Janine said wryly. 'I told him if he wouldn't do it, I would. When he realised I meant it he gave in. Exposing a family disagreement in public—well…'

'It would have made people laugh at him,' Harriet said. 'And he couldn't have that. You know, marrying you was the best thing that ever happened to Amos. You're the only person who can make him stop his nonsense.'

'Shh!' Janine put a finger to her lips. 'Never tell him I told you.'

'It's a promise.'

A cheer from outside put them all on alert.

'Travis,' Harriet said at once. 'When you hear them cheering you know it's Travis. I'll bet he's blowing kisses to them, putting his arms around girls in the crowd.'

'Not if Charlene's with him,' Janine observed.

'He's almost paranoid about considering her feelings.'

'And the joke is that it doesn't bother her,' Darius observed. 'He can do as he likes because Charlene knows she's got him just where she wants him.'

'Sounds the perfect arrangement to me,' said his wife.

'And you should know,' he said, smiling at her. 'You snap your fingers and I jump to attention, don't I?'

The look they shared seemed to sum up the air of joyful contentment that permeated the whole family these days. One by one the sons had found wives who were perfect for them.

Darius had turned his back on the society women who would gladly have been his to marry Harriet, a girl from the island he owned. Marcel had rediscovered love with Cassie, a woman he'd once known and lost. Travis had sought Charlene's protection against an intrusive press, only to find that his need of her went further and deeper than he could have dreamed. And Leonid's love for Perdita had survived quarrels and misunderstandings because their union had been fated from the moment they met.

Only one son was left: Jackson, who had introduced Freya to Dan Connor, the man she would marry today.

'Does anyone know anything about the groom?' Harriet asked.

'He owns a big television production company,' Travis explained. 'His documentaries made Jackson a star.'

'It's nearly time for things to start happening,' Janine said.

'Yes,' Travis agreed. 'We ought to take our places. I thought Dan and Jackson would have been here by now. I wonder what's keeping them.'

'Aren't you ready yet?' Jackson called through the half-open door of the bedroom. 'The car's downstairs.'

'I'm here,' Dan said, appearing. 'Just a few last-minute things to get right.'

The mirror threw back a reflection of two men in their thirties, both tall and handsome, both dressed for a wedding.

Jackson was the better looking, with a quick,

teasing smile that could transform him. Observers sometimes said that of all Amos Falcon's sons he most resembled him. His lean face and firm features came from the same mould as his father. Amos's white hair had once been light brown, as Jackson's still was, and their eyes were an identical deep blue.

The differences between them were subtle. A lifetime of demanding his own way and usually getting it had given Amos's face a harsh, set look, as though it rested on stone. The same features in Jackson were gentler, as perhaps his father's had been many years ago. Only the future would determine how much closer the resemblance would one day grow.

'Do I look all right?' Dan demanded, studying himself in the mirror.

'You look fine to me,' Jackson said, grinning. 'The perfect picture of a deliriously happy groom.'

Dan threw him a withering look. 'Just shut it, will you? There's no such thing as a deliriously happy groom. We're all shaking with nerves at the plunge we're about to take.'

'Come to think of it, you're right,' Jackson

mused. 'My brothers were all on edge at their weddings—at least until they got their brides safely riveted. Then they relaxed.'

But even as he said it he knew there was something more behind Dan's tension. Dan was in his prime, wealthy, and with a streak of confidence that seemed to infuse his whole life. It had helped him build up Connor Productions, known for its colourful documentaries. It had also carried him through many affairs of the heart, which he'd survived by being wary of commitment.

But when Jackson had introduced him to Freya that wariness had begun to desert him, until suddenly, without warning, he'd made a determined and forceful proposal. Jackson knew that because he'd been sitting two tables away in the same restaurant, and had clearly heard Dan say, 'That's it! My mind's made up. You've simply got to marry me.'

Freya had given the rich chuckle that was one of her attractions, and teased, 'Oh, I've got to, have I?'

'Definitely. It's all settled. You're going to be Mrs Connor.'

He'd slipped a hand behind her head, drawing

her close for a kiss, untroubled by the crowd of other diners who'd laughed and applauded. The next day he'd bought her a diamond ring, and celebrations had commenced.

Jackson was glad for both of them. Freya had been his stepsister for six years. Their relationship might be called 'jumpy'. Sometimes they were cordial, and sometimes she challenged him.

'Who are you to give me orders?' she'd demanded once.

'I wasn't—'

'Yes, you were. You don't even know you're doing it. You're just like your father.'

'That's a terrible thing to say!'

'Why? I thought you admired him.'

'Some of the time,' he'd replied wryly. 'I don't like his way of giving orders without even realising he's doing it. But that doesn't mean I'm like him, and don't you dare say I am.'

'Oh, yeah?'

'Yeah.'

'Yeah?'

'Yeah!'

And their sparring had ended in laughter, as it so often did.

He thought fondly of her now—a sensible girl with brains enough to have passed her nursing degree with top marks, who could yet enjoy a squabble and give as good as she got. She would never be a great beauty, but her looks were agreeable. Dan had chosen well, he reckoned.

Almost at once after their engagement he'd had to leave to film a documentary on the other side of the world. He'd returned a week before the wedding and seen that his friend was on edge. He'd attached little importance to this, considering it standard bridegroom stuff. Even Dan's heavy drinking on his stag night had not alarmed him. It had merely underlined his duty to get Dan safely through the ceremony.

'Come on,' he said, opening the front door. 'Time to go.'

'Just a moment,' Dan said quickly. 'There's something—'

'Stop panicking. I've got it.'

'Got—?'

'The ring. Look.' Jackson reached into his pocket for a small box, which he opened to reveal a gold ring. 'That's what you were getting worked up about, wasn't it?'

'Of course. Of course.'

The tension in Dan's voice made Jackson regard him kindly and clap him on the shoulder. 'Everything's all right,' he said. 'Nothing can go wrong now. Time to go.'

In moments they were downstairs, greeting the chauffeur, settling into the back seat of the car.

It wasn't a long journey to the church but the traffic was heavy that morning. As they crawled along at a snail's pace Jackson gave a sigh of frustration.

'Come on,' he groaned. 'If it takes any longer, Dad and Freya will turn up before we do.'

'Is Amos really giving her away? I can't get my head round that.'

'Why shouldn't he? Oh, you mean because he wanted her to marry one of his own sons? When Leonid married Perdita there was only me left, and I told him to forget it. I like Freya, but not in that way.'

'I guess that's why you introduced me to her? Hoping I'd do what you wouldn't?'

'It wasn't like that,' Jackson said, shocked. 'Of course I was glad for her to know as many

other guys as possible, but I wasn't making secret plans.'

'Aw, come on. You were hoping the old man
would admit defeat. No way. He moved heaven
and earth to stop this wedding.'

'What the devil do you mean by that?'

'When I was going out with Freya he came to
see me. He wanted to warn me off. Said I should
leave her alone, and if I didn't—well, there were
a few hints about the damage he could do to me
financially.'

'But you told him to get stuffed?'

'I didn't say anything. No chance. He said his
piece and walked out, slamming the door. I guess
he just took it for granted that I'd do as he said.'

'Yes,' Jackson murmured. 'He has a way of
doing that. He scares people. But not you. You
stood up to him and proposed to her. Good for
you. She's a lucky girl to have a guy who loves
her so much.'

'But I'm not in love with her,' Dan said explosively. 'I lost my temper, that's all. I'm damned
if I'll let any man give me orders. Sorry, I know
he's your father—'

'That's all right,' Jackson said hastily. 'But are

you telling me you only proposed to Freya because you were angry? I don't believe it.'

'Believe it. I just saw red. But then suddenly we
were engaged and—hell, I don't know. She's a
nice girl, but I'm not in love, and if Amos hadn't
tried to scare me out of proposing I'd never have
done it.'

'I don't believe this,' Jackson said frantically. 'I
was there at your engagement party, and if ever
I saw two people in love—'

'Yes, I played the devoted lover—and you know
why? Because Amos was there, looking fit to do
murder. Oh, brother, did I enjoy that!'

'But he's giving her away.'

'I reckon his wife twisted his arm. Freya's her
daughter and she wouldn't want him making
trouble.'

Jackson tore at his hair.

'Let me understand this,' he said, aghast.
'You've let things get this far, and you're really
saying you're not in love with the girl you're
about to marry?'

'That's right. I'm not. But what can I do? She's
obviously in love with me and I'm trapped. I can

feel the noose tightening around my neck with every moment.'

'You should have been honest with her before this,' Jackson said furiously. 'Now you'll hurt her a lot more if you marry her without love and let her down later.'

In his agitated state Jackson spoke instinctively. Afterwards he was to curse himself for a fool, but by then it was too late.

'That's true,' Dan said, staring at him as though a light had suddenly dawned. 'And there's still time to put things right.'

As he spoke the car halted at traffic lights. Dan opened the door and began to ease himself out.

'You go on to the church,' he said. 'Explain why I'm not with you. Make them realise I had no choice.'

'*What?* Don't be daft. You've got to go through with it now.'

'I can't. You've just made me understand that.'

'Dan! Don't you dare— Come back.'

But Dan had slammed the door and begun to run.

'Wait here,' Jackson told the chauffeur, scrambling out of the car. 'Dan! Come back. *Come back.*'

But Dan was running fast, darting in and out of the traffic which had started to move again. He reached the other side of the road and vanished down an alley. Jackson raced after him as fast as he could, nearly being hit by a car. But when he reached the street it was empty.

'Dan!' he yelled. 'You can't do this. *Please!*'

There was no answer.

'Where are you?' he cried. 'Don't hide from me. Let's talk.'

He tore along the road, searching everywhere but without result.

'I didn't mean it!' he shouted. 'Not the way it came out. I spoke without thinking but I never meant— Don't do this.'

He ran up and down for a few more minutes before facing facts.

'Oh, no!' he groaned. 'This can't be happening. But it is, and I'm to blame. It'll be my fault if— Oh, what have I done? *What have I done?*'

Windows were opening above him. He made a hasty exit, returning to the car and throwing himself into the back seat. 'Go on to the church,' he growled.

At last the building came in sight, and he groaned again as he saw the excited crowds and the cameras.

'Not here,' he said hastily. 'Go around the back.'

He slid down low, hoping not to be seen, and didn't sit up again until they reached the back of the church. He paid the chauffeur, adding a generous tip and putting his finger over his lips. Then he hurried through a rear door as fast as he could.

In seven years of making documentaries Jackson had many times had to screw up his courage. He'd faced lions, swum in dangerously deep water, and talked into cameras from great heights. But none of those things had made his stomach churn as much as the thought of the next few minutes.

He tried to tell himself that Freya would cope well. She was a trained nurse and a strong, efficient, determined young woman, not a wilting violet. But a voice in his mind wouldn't let him get away with that.

You're just telling yourself what you want to be-

lieve. This is going to devastate her, and it's your fault, so stop trying to make it easy on yourself.

As he slipped quietly into the main body of the church he saw the family gathered in the front pews. Travis looked up and gestured for him to approach.

'What's up?' he asked as Jackson neared. 'Where's the groom?'

'He's not coming. He changed his mind at the last minute and dashed out of the car. I tried to follow but I lost sight of him.'

'What do you mean?' demanded Janine. 'He can't just dump my daughter with the wedding about to start.'

'I'm afraid that's what he's done. It seems he's always had doubts and suddenly they crushed him.'

Before anyone could say more the organ burst into the melody of 'Here Comes The Bride.'

'Oh, no!' Jackson groaned.

'There they are,' said Darius. 'Oh, heavens. What a disaster!'

Everyone stared to the end of the aisle, where Amos could clearly be seen with Freya on his arm. Jackson cursed himself for his clumsiness.

He should have waited outside for the car and told them the truth there. Then Freya could have returned home at once, without having to make the humiliating trip down the aisle.

He thought of hurrying forward, approaching her now before she came any closer, but she was already in the spotlight. Or at least Amos was. People recognised him. Some waved to him. Some slipped into the aisle to greet him. Jackson had no choice but to wait, suffering agonies of impatience, his eyes fixed on Freya.

For a moment he almost believed that this was somebody else. The strong, sensible young woman who lived in his mind had vanished, replaced by a girl in a glamorous white satin dress. Her fair hair, normally straight, had been curled into an exotic creation and covered by a lace veil that trailed down almost to the floor.

There was a glow about her that he'd never seen before. She was smiling as though fate had brought her to a blissful destination. It made her look exactly as a happy bride ought to look, and Jackson closed his eyes, sickened by what was about to happen.

As they neared him and saw that Jackson was alone, Amos began to frown.

'Where's the groom?' he rasped. 'Why isn't he with you?'

'Shh!' Freya silenced him with a finger over her lips. 'He must have slipped away to the Gents. He'll be here in a moment.' She gave Jackson a teasing smile. 'I expect he had a bit too much to drink last night, didn't he?'

Her good nature was almost too much for him to bear. How could Dan not have wanted to marry this sweet creature?

'I'm afraid there's been a problem,' he said in a low voice. 'Dan isn't here. He's—he's not coming.'

'What do you mean?' Freya asked. 'Is he ill? Oh, heavens, I must go to him.'

'No, he's not ill,' Jackson said. 'I'm sorry, Freya, but he changed his mind at the last minute. He got out of the car and ran. I don't even know where he is now.'

'He ran?' Freya whispered. 'To get away from me? Oh, no!' She withdrew her hand from Amos's arm and faced Jackson. 'But why?'

'He lost his nerve,' Jackson said uneasily.

The words seemed to swirl in Freya's head, meaningless yet full of monstrous meaning.

'What—what do you mean—lost his nerve?' she stammered. 'It doesn't take nerve to—to—'

To marry someone you love. The words were on the tip of her tongue, yet some power stopped her from saying them.

Jackson understood and struggled for an answer.

'It's a big occasion,' he managed. 'Some men can't cope.'

But Dan was used to big occasions, and they both knew it. Freya's look of disbelief told Jackson he'd have to do better than that.

'Why?' she said fiercely. 'What really happened?'

'He just—couldn't cope suddenly.'

Freya swung away from him, trying to cope with the feelings that stormed through her. Pain, disbelief, disillusion, humiliation all fought for supremacy. Humiliation won.

Dan had charmed her, filled her grey world with light and made her feel special—the kind of woman that other women envied. Now he was knocking her down in the eyes of the world. She clenched her hands into fists, holding them up against her eyes and emitting a soft groan.

Behind her Jackson said, 'Freya—' reaching out to touch her, but she pulled away.

'I'm all right,' she said, dropping her hands.

He didn't believe it for a moment, but he respected her determination to appear strong.

Amos was in a stew, growling, 'Just let me get my hands on him.'

It was on the tip of Jackson's tongue to hurl a bitter accusation at his father, telling him how his actions had been the trigger. With a huge effort at control he fought back the words for Freya's sake.

A murmur was rising from the congregation as they sensed trouble. The vicar drew close and spoke quietly.

'Perhaps you'd like to come into the back and talk privately?'

Amos reached out to take Freya's hand but Jackson was there first, slipping his arm around her and leading her away to where there were no curious eyes. The family followed them.

When they were safely in the back room Jackson repeated the story, keeping hold of Freya's hand, feeling the terrible stillness that had settled over her.

'Why did he do it?' she whispered. 'What did he say?'

'Only that when he came to the point—he just couldn't,' Jackson prevaricated, wishing the earth would swallow him up.

'I'll kill him,' Amos muttered.

'Join the queue,' Travis said. 'We'll all enjoy doing that.'

'No,' Freya said. 'This is for me to take care of. I must speak to him. I need a phone.'

'Not now,' Jackson said quickly.

'Yes, now,' she said.

Darius produced a cell phone. Freya reached for it but Jackson got there first, seizing her wrist and shaking his head to make his brother back off.

'Let go of me,' she said. 'Darius—'

But Darius had read the dark message in Jackson's eyes.

'He's right, Freya,' he admitted. 'Not just now. Give yourself a moment first.'

She turned furious eyes on Jackson.

'You've got a nerve. Who are you to tell me what to do?'

'I'm your stepbrother who's concerned about you,' he said firmly.

'And who thinks he can dictate to me. Give me that phone. I must talk to Dan.'

'Wait. Let me try.'

He didn't know what he was trying to achieve by speaking to Dan first. The situation was already a car wreck. But he took out his own cell phone and dialled the number. There was only silence.

Freya lost patience, seizing the phone from him and dialling again. Still there was no response. She closed her eyes, feeling as though she was surrounded by an infinity in which there was neither light nor sound. Only nothingness. At last she gave up. Her shoulders sagged.

'He's turned his phone off,' she said bleakly. 'He really is running away from me. I've got to get out of here. How can I find a way out through the back? I can't go back down the aisle with everyone watching.'

'Come on,' Jackson said, taking her arm before anyone else in the family could do so and leading her out.

To his relief an exit soon appeared. But his relief was short-lived. His arrival without Dan had been seen and the word had already gone round, both in the congregation and the waiting press. People were gathering at the back of the church, alive with curiosity. When Freya appeared a cry went up.

'There she is! What happened? Where's the groom?'

'Get away!' Jackson yelled. 'Leave her alone.'

He got in front of her, waving his hands to force them back.

'It's all right,' he said, turning back to her. 'Freya—Freya?'

She had gone, running away down the street in a way that ironically echoed Dan's escape. For the second time that day Jackson gave chase, this time catching up easily.

'Go away,' she cried. 'Leave me alone.'

She turned and would have run again but he seized her shoulders.

'Let me go.'

'Freya, I can't do that. Heaven knows what would happen to you. I'm not taking that risk.'

'It's my risk, nobody else's,' she cried. 'Do you think I care?'

'No, but I care.'

'Let me go!'

'*No!* I've said no and I mean no, so stop arguing. *Taxi!*'

By great good luck one had appeared. He hustled her inside, gave the driver the address of the hotel where the family was staying, then got into the back and took her into his arms.

'Let it out,' he said. 'Cry if you want to.'

'I'm not going to cry,' she declared. *'I'm all right.'*

But as he held her he knew she was far from all right, perhaps not weeping but shaking violently. He drew her close to him, patting her shoulder but saying nothing. Words would not help now. He could only offer friendship, knowing that even that was feeble against the blow that had struck her.

At last she looked up and he saw her face, pale and devastated.

'I'm here,' he said. 'Hold onto me.'

Even as he said it he felt foolish. Yes, he was there, the person whose clumsiness had helped to bring about this disaster. But there was nothing else to say.

At last the hotel came in sight, and at once he knew he had another calamity on his hands. The front was crowded with people watching the street for interesting arrivals.

'Oh, no!' he groaned. 'The word's got out already.'

'And they're waiting for me to come crawling back,' she said. 'Look, someone's got a camera.'

'Then they're going to be disappointed,' Jackson said grimly. 'Driver, there's been a change of plan.' He gave his own address and the car swerved away.

'They'll never find us at my place,' he said. 'You can stay until you're safe.'

'Thank you,' she whispered. 'But will I ever be safe again?'

'You will be. I'll see to it. Just hold me. Everything's going to be all right.'

If only he could believe it.

CHAPTER TWO

AT LAST THEY reached the apartment block where Jackson lived, and managed to slip inside unseen. It took a few moments to go up in the elevator, and there was his front door.

'Now we're safe,' he said, closing it behind them. 'Forget them. They can't get at you here.'

Freya looked around her as though confused, but suddenly she stopped, staring at a mirror on the wall. She was still wearing her veil and the pearl tiara that held it in place. With a gasp of fury she seized them, ripping them off and hurling them to the floor. Then she seized at her hair, tearing down the elaborate coiffure until it hung untidily about her face.

'I've got to get out of this dress,' she cried.

'Come in here,' Jackson said, leading her into his bedroom and opening the wardrobe. 'Put something of mine on. My clothes will be too big for you, but they'll do for a while. I'll leave you.'

'Wait.' She turned so that her back was towards him. 'I can't undo it alone.'

There seemed to be a thousand tiny buttons to be released, and Jackson went to work. It wasn't the first time he'd helped a woman undress, but those experiences were no use to him now. Inch by inch her figure came into view, and inwardly he cursed Dan again for abandoning such delicate beauty.

'Thank you,' she said at last. 'I can manage the rest for myself.'

'I'll be outside if you want me,' he said, and hurried away.

Left alone, Freya freed herself from the dress and the slip beneath. In the wardrobe she found a pair of jeans and a shirt, which she slipped on, and then she looked at herself in the full-length mirror.

It was only a short time ago that she'd stared at herself in the glamorous dress, hardly daring to believe that the beauty gazing back was actually herself.

'And I shouldn't have believed it,' she murmured. 'This is the real me—the one I always knew I was. Dull, ordinary. Not too bad on a good day, but pretty dreary on a bad one. I guess all the days are going to be bad from now on, and if I'm wise I'll stick to working clothes.'

For several minutes she stood there, trying to get used to this other self, stranded in a bleak world.

In his office Jackson made a hurried phone call to Janine at the hotel.

'Just to let you know that Freya's all right,' he told her. 'I've brought her home with me.'

'Oh, Jackson, thank you!' she exclaimed. 'There are such rows going on. Amos is fit to do murder. So are your brothers.'

'I thought so. Freya needs to be well away from that. Don't worry, I'll keep her safe.'

'How kind you are. She's so lucky to have you!'

He gave a silent groan. If Janine knew the full story she'd be saying something very different. It was no use telling himself that he was essentially innocent. Dan had been seeking something that would trigger him into action and Jackson's thoughtless words had done the trick. Now the beautiful bride was alone and humiliated, staring into an empty future.

'Ask her to call me when she can,' Janine said. 'But as long as she's with you I know she's all right.'

He made a polite reply and hung up. For a moment he stayed tense and still, wishing he was anywhere in the universe but here. The click of the door made him look behind him to see Freya, clad in jeans and shirt, bearing no resemblance to the dazzling creature who'd come down the aisle in expectation of bliss.

'Come on,' he said. 'Let's have something to eat. There's a Chinese restaurant nearby that delivers. You like king prawns with black pepper, don't you?'

'Yes, but how did you know?'

'It was the first thing I learned about you when we met six years ago. My father and your mother were just beginning to talk about marriage and the four of us had an evening out in a restaurant. But then some of Dad's business contacts turned up and he simply forgot about the rest of us.'

'We made a run for it,' she remembered. 'There was a Chinese place a few yards away.'

'And we had a good time there,' he said. 'Lots of laughs. Right—prawns it is.'

He made the call and the food arrived a few minutes later. Briefly they were both absorbed in serving it and getting settled at the table, but then she uttered the words he'd been dreading.

'Jackson, I want you to tell me what really happened.'

'But I've told you—'

'I mean the bits you've left out. Oh, please don't pretend you didn't. What you said in the church was the polite version. It had to be, with all those people listening, but I really need to know. Dan got this far and then he suddenly backed off. There has to be a reason, and I think I know what it is, but I need to hear you say it.'

'You—know what it is?' he said cautiously.

'Are you afraid I won't be able to cope? Don't worry. I'm not going to burst into tears and weep all over you. But, however painful the truth is, knowing it is better than wondering. Was it something I did wrong?'

'No, nothing like that.'

'Then I guess I know the answer, and I can see why you don't want to tell me.'

'Can you?' he said with growing alarm.

'Well it's obvious, isn't it? Something happened

to make him realise that he couldn't go through with it.'

'Don't—jump to conclusions,' he said uneasily while his mind whirled. Surely she couldn't have guessed what had really happened?

'There's only one thing it can be.' She took a deep breath. 'When you were on the way to the church you and he got talking and—and—'

'And what?' he forced himself to say, inwardly cowering.

'He told you he's in love with someone else, didn't he?'

Jackson's relief was so great that he nearly dropped his spoon. Perhaps he was going to get off more lightly than he deserved.

'I think she must have called him before he left,' Freya went on. 'And on the journey he realised that he loved her too much to marry me.'

'No, he didn't say anything like that. He just lost his nerve.'

'Oh, please, I know you're being kind, but this isn't the moment for kindness. It's the moment for truth, however brutal. There's another woman, isn't there?'

'Not that I know about,' he said firmly. 'But if

that were the answer isn't it better for you to escape him now? If you'd found out after you were married it would have been a bigger disaster.'

'Would it? Perhaps I might have seen her off. If he'd chosen me over her—'

'Freya, listen to me. If a man can act like this on the way to his wedding then he's only interested in himself and you're better off without him.'

'Maybe I'll feel like that one day.' She sighed. 'But it's hard to imagine now. I'll always remember how it felt to walk down the aisle, looking for Dan, sure that he'd be watching for me. I was so happy—and such a fool. When you came towards us I was delighted to see you. But then—there was nothing but emptiness. I was going to build my life around Dan, and suddenly there's no life to build. Oh, I'm sorry. I promised I wouldn't embarrass you.'

'I'm not embarrassed. Say anything you want to. But listen to me. One life may have vanished, but there'll be another one—and it will be better.'

She gave a slightly hysterical laugh. 'You think I should be glad this happened?'

'Not right now, but in years to come you'll see that it was for the best that you got rid of him.'

'But I didn't. He got rid of me. He threw me aside like a piece of unwanted waste.'

'You mustn't think like that. You're worth a thousand of Dan. How could you ever have thought yourself in love with him?'

'Because right from the first moment I knew he was going to be special to me. My whole life changed just because he existed. It was as though the world had suddenly opened up. And everything was different—more exciting, more wonderful. When he proposed to me I was sure I'd never be unhappy again.'

Jackson drew a long, hard breath. It would be so simple now to tell her that Dan's proposal had just been a defiance of Amos. But her heart had already been broken once, and he flinched from the thought of breaking it again.

'He let you down,' he growled. 'He's not the man you thought him.'

'And I'm not the woman he really wanted. I can't hide from that. But I'll survive—with your help. Thanks for everything today.' She made a wry face. 'Even the bits that made me mad at you.'

'Sorry I had to come on so strong. I didn't want to pull you around, but—'

'I didn't give you any choice, did I? If you'd let me run off down the road—well, where would I be now? I'll swear you're the best brother I've ever had.'

'Since you don't have *any* brothers I'm not sure how to take that.'

They laughed together, both sounding shaky.

'And just think of the price you're going to pay.' She sighed again. 'This is going to give Amos ideas again.'

'About pairing us off, you mean? I guess so, but don't worry. You have nothing to fear from me.' He took her hand and assumed a theatrical tone. 'Freya, I give you my word, nothing will ever make me marry you. Let thunderbolts and lightning descend, I will still declare: *Not her. Anyone but her.*'

'Just be sure you say it to Amos and make it convincing.'

'You too. We'll have to persuade him that we can't stand the sight of each other.'

'I'll try, but it'll be hard. Right this minute you look like the nicest man in the world.'

'That's a delusion,' he said self-consciously.

'If you say so.'

'I do say so. If you knew what a swine I really am you'd sock me in the jaw.'

'Another time. Right now I have something else to ask of you.' She slipped a hand into the jeans pocket and brought out the luscious engagement ring that she had worn until a few hours ago. 'Will you give that back to Dan, please?'

'Oh, heavens, now I remember. I've still got the other ring.'

He reached into his jacket pocket and took out the wedding ring, laying the two of them side by side on the table.

'I'll give these to him as soon as I see him.'

She didn't reply. She was gazing at the rings as though transfixed. After a moment she brushed a hand over her eyes, but not soon enough to hide the tears.

'I'm sorry, I just—'

'You've endured enough,' he said sympathetically. 'Why don't you go and lie down? I won't disturb you. The bedroom's yours. I'll sleep out here on the sofa.'

'Why are you so kind to me?' she choked.

Because I feel guilty for what I accidentally did to you.

The words thrummed through his head, almost forcing their way out. But he controlled them and escorted her into the bedroom.

'You'll find some clean pyjamas in that drawer,' he said, and hurried out before his conscience overwhelmed him.

Left alone, she sat down on the bed, staring into space, unable to find the strength for anything else. In Jackson's company, feeling his kindly care, she'd managed to cope. But now she felt as though she was drifting through infinity, in a world in which nothing was real.

She had tried to describe how Dan had made her feel, but there were no words for the sensation of being newly alive that he had given her. For the first time in her life she'd felt valuable to someone. Her relationship with her mother was cordial, but she knew she'd never come first. Janine and her late father had adored each other with an intensity that had made Freya feel like an outsider.

She'd made a life for herself, training as a nurse and passing her exams with honours. She'd had the pleasure of knowing that her parents were proud of her—especially her father, a learned man, who had been delighted that his brains had passed to his daughter. That had to be her consolation for the feeling of having been outside the enchanted circle.

Her loneliness had been intensified when her father died. Mother and daughter had grieved, but not together. Janine had suffered mostly alone, in a place Freya had not been able to touch.

But she was a successful nurse, and life had seemed settled on a conventional path until, two years after her father's death, her mother had become engaged to the notorious Amos Falcon and she had begun to meet his five sons.

Jackson had been the first, on that evening in the restaurant that he'd mentioned earlier. Their escape to the nearby Chinese restaurant had been merry, but there had been another feeling beneath her laughter. He was handsome, charming, and she wouldn't have minded if he'd asked her out on a date.

He hadn't. She had sighed, shrugged, and returned to the young man she'd been dating, but who had suddenly seemed less interesting. They'd drifted apart.

At last there had been the wedding of Janine and Amos in London, and a gathering of the whole family in a hotel the night before. Jackson had greeted her with a cry of, 'There's my little sister!' and enfolded her in a huge hug.

They'd moved away from the others to chat about how their lives were going. That had been before his television career, when he'd still been a newspaper journalist, with a thousand fascinating tales to tell. Freya had listened, promising herself that this time she would attract his interest. She'd already discovered how much he liked to laugh.

'Go on—tell me more,' she'd teased. 'I'm hanging on every word.'

'Hey, I really like talking to you.' He had chuckled. 'You know how to flatter a guy's vanity. Why don't we—?' He'd stopped, riveted by something he'd seen over her shoulder. 'Hey, look who's— *Karen!*'

Then he'd been gone, racing across the room to the girl who'd just appeared, seizing her in his arms, kissing her again and again.

'So she turned up after all,' a voice had said in Freya's ear. 'We all wondered if she would.'

It had been Darius, regarding his brother with good-humoured cynicism.

'Who is she?' Freya had asked casually.

'His latest light o' love.'

'Latest?'

'They come and they go. Jackson likes variety in his life, which is partly why they broke up. Now they've got back together we'll have to wait and see what happens.'

'No prizes for guessing what's about to happen now,' Freya had observed, watching the pair slip out of the room.

'He wouldn't be Jackson if he passed up the chance.'

It was a lucky escape, she'd told herself. She might have become seriously attracted to Jackson but fate had saved her.

He'd brought Karen to the wedding as his guest.

She was beautiful, Freya had thought enviously. Others had thought so too, because at the reception another man hadn't been able to take his eyes from her. He'd hovered, annoying Karen, until Jackson had taken a firm grip on him and said something that had made him back off. Freya hadn't heard the words but she'd seen Jackson's face, and there had been a look of menace that had stunned her. All the charm had gone from him.

It had been over in a moment. The man had fled and Jackson had reverted to his usual pleasant self. But Freya had never forgotten what she had glimpsed. She knew that if anyone had looked at her like that she would have been terrified.

She'd expected to hear that Jackson was engaged to Karen, but nothing had happened. And why should she care? she wondered. She'd been briefly attracted to him, but rescue had come in time and it was no big deal. They'd settled for a friendship in which they teased, challenged and infuriated each other. What might have been was safely in the past.

There was still a sense of irony that of all men it should be Jackson who had come to her rescue now, taking her into his home, offering her his shoulder to cry on. But irony had always been part of their relationship.

Early in her mother's marriage she'd joined Amos and Janine at their home in Monte Carlo. A heart attack had left him vulnerable, and Janine had asked her to pay a long visit.

'He won't hear of a nurse being there night and day,' she'd said. 'But he'll have to let my daughter visit us, won't he?'

She'd made the visit reluctantly. Nothing about Amos appealed to her, especially the stories of his several wives and affairs. But Amos had taken a liking to his stepdaughter and begun plotting to marry her to one of his sons. Freya had been far from flattered.

'Was he mad when he thought of that?' she'd demanded of her mother. 'There isn't one of them I'd ever dream of—ye gods and little fishes!'

As soon as Amos's health had improved she'd left Monte Carlo, returning to England and her nursing career.

Amos had failed to marry her to Darius, Marcel, Travis or Leonid. That left only Jackson. Their friendship was strong enough for him to 'reject' her theatrically, as he'd just done. Since she felt the same there was no problem.

She'd be as mad to marry him as he'd be to marry her. Though there was no denying he was a nice enough guy—at least he was if you overlooked a few things—but he was a bit too set on having his own way. He must get that from Amos, although he'd never admit it. But he had been good to her today.

She pulled on the pyjamas he'd offered her and lay down on the bed, certain that she would be unable to sleep, but the strain of the day caught up with her suddenly and she could do nothing but close her eyes.

Jackson spent the next couple of hours quietly, so as not to disturb Freya. There was research that needed to be done for his next documentary, but somehow it was hard to imagine himself continuing to work with Dan. Professionally they had both benefited from working together, which made their relationship cordial without being an outright friendship.

He considered calling his father but decided against it. After what he'd learned this afternoon he was afraid he might speak his mind too bluntly. He had things to say to Amos about his behaviour, but he'd rather say them face to face.

The old man's determination to make Freya his daughter-in-law had been a source of comedy and irritation in equal measure to his five sons. Their amusement had been good-natured, helped by the fact that Freya was no keener on the idea than they were.

If anything it had seemed to put the brothers and Freya off each other. There was no denying that Jackson found her a nice, attractive girl, but he'd never really thought of Freya that way, and nor had his brothers. She'd been Amos's 'tool'— an instrument for his bullying. He briefly wondered whether Freya had ever fancied *any* of them.

No way. Unless—

A faint memory came back to him: the evening in the Chinese restaurant. They had laughed and exchanged significant glances as couples did at the start, when their attraction was in the flickering, questioning stage. But the pressure from Amos had begun soon afterwards and he'd backed off, sensing with relief that Freya was doing the same. After that each had known the other was out of bounds.

But if Amos's clumsiness hadn't come between them what would have happened? Until now he'd never really wondered.

Quietly he went to the bedroom door and opened it just a crack. From inside he could hear the sound of soft breathing. He opened it a little further, enough to catch a faint glimpse of her lying on the bed.

Freya wasn't the only woman who'd slept in that bed. It was large enough for two people, and he used it for what he thought of as 'entertaining'. Many women had lain there, skimpily dressed or undressed. They'd looked at him through half-closed eyes, pretending to sleep while actually studying him, planning their next move.

But Freya's form was totally concealed by his pyjamas. Her eyes were closed and the faint sounds she made told him that she was sunk in the sleep of exhaustion. She looked like a vul-nerable child. He was heart-stricken. And he was floundering, baffled about how to cope. It was a new experience—one that alarmed him.

Quietly he closed the door and went to switch

on the television. Almost at once he heard the words 'Dan Connor'.

The screen was focussed on a film première. There were the stars, walking along the red carpet, and there was a luscious young female clutching the arm of her escort. Dan Connor.

'*There's* someone we didn't expect to see,' declared the presenter. 'Dan Connor, television bigshot. He should have got married today, but—hey, Dan, what happened?'

'Life happened,' Dan declared, grinning in a way that made Jackson want to commit murder. 'Apart from that—no comment.' He leered at the girl on his arm. 'Shall we go in?'

Jackson clenched his hands, silently calling Dan every name he could think of. He moved quickly to turn the set off, but it was too late. A faint sound made him look to see Freya standing in the doorway.

'So that's who she is,' Freya said quietly.

'No. Freya, you're wrong. I'll swear he's not in love with her. He must have just grabbed the first girl he met so that he could get his face onto the news. That's a PR stunt you're witnessing. You've had a lucky escape.'

She smiled at him, calm and seemingly untroubled.

'You may be right. He replaced me easily, didn't he? At any rate it's all over now. As far as I'm concerned Dan never existed. Goodnight.'

She retreated into the bedroom, leaving Jackson wishing he could believe that she was really recovering so easily. But his heart told him she was only putting on a brave face.

Before going to bed he listened outside her door and heard something that made him clench his hands in agony. From inside came the sound of gasping sobs, telling all too clearly of the grief Freya could only release when she was alone.

Unable to endure it, he opened the door, ready to go in, take her in his arms and comfort her. But wisdom held him back. She wouldn't be glad of his comfort. She would hate it, wanting no curious eyes.

He backed out and closed the door, knowing that he wasn't wanted.

Freya awoke early the next morning. Briefly she wondered where she was, then remembered and groaned. Creeping out of the room, she searched for Jackson on the sofa, but it was empty except for a scrap of paper that read, *I'll be back soon. Don't go away.*

She thought of the hotel, where the family was staying, and knew she should return to them, but the thought made her shudder.

If only Jackson were here. She'd always considered herself a strong person, but suddenly it seemed terrible to be alone.

'That's his fault for supporting me so well,' she muttered wryly. 'Now I can't cope without him. All his fault. Oh, where is he?'

It was an hour before he returned and it seemed like for ever.

'I've been to the hotel,' he said, dumping a large suitcase on the table. 'I took the wedding dress with me and your mother's going to pack it away for you. She gave me some clothes to bring you.'

Her wedding dress had been hanging up in the bedroom, which meant he must have crept in and removed it while she was asleep. Then her attention was taken by the clothes she found in the case.

'Why did you bring this?' she asked, lifting a glittering cocktail dress.

'You can wear it tonight, when we go out.'

'Are we going out?'

'Yes. I'll take you back to your hotel at the end of the evening, but before that we need to give Dan a taste of his own medicine. He flaunted himself before the cameras, so you have to do the same. Then everyone will know you don't give a stuff about him.'

'Don't I?'

'No, you don't. You mustn't. I know what I'm doing, Freya. Trust me.'

'I do,' she said.

'But you think I'm giving you orders again, don't you? Laying down the law, acting like my father?'

'No, he never takes so much trouble about people's feelings,' she said. 'I don't mind taking a few orders from you.'

'What was that? Did I hear you right? My bolshie Freya being meek and mild? I don't believe it.'

'I can do meek and mild if there's a good reason.' She managed a smile. 'I can even say, *Yes, sir. No, sir. Three bags full, sir.*'

'This I have to see,' he said dramatically. 'It'll

be a whole new experience.' Then abruptly he dropped the humorous manner. 'Don't worry. I just mean to look after you.' He took her face between his hands. 'That's all that matters now. Please believe me.'

'I do,' she said. 'It's strange how content I feel to leave everything in your hands. I didn't know it before, but there's nobody I trust like you.'

To her surprise Jackson looked uneasy, but she thought she understood. He was more used to her sparring with him than trusting him. But now those days seemed a long way off.

CHAPTER THREE

NOW FREYA REALLY discovered Jackson's flair for taking charge. In the suitcase she found items of make-up and for hair care, evidently packed by her mother.

'Thank goodness,' she said. 'At least I can look my best tonight.'

But he shook his head.

'Tonight you're a star,' he said, 'and a star doesn't do those jobs herself. She employs a professional.'

'You mean a beautician? I don't know any.'

'But I do. She'll arrive this afternoon, to place herself at your service.' He hesitated before adding, 'Unless, that is, you have any objections?'

Her lips twitched. 'Don't worry. I know the proper answer to that. Yes, sir. No, sir.'

'You forgot *Three bags full, sir*. But I'll let you off this time. I've got to leave now, but I'll be back this evening.'

Naomi, the beautician, arrived at three in the afternoon. She listened politely to what Freya had to say, but clearly needed no instructions, having already received them from Jackson.

It was ironic that once Freya would have objected to the way he was directing every step. But now the sadness that consumed her made it hard to think, and it was a relief to leave the decisions to him.

She had to admit that Naomi did a magnificent job, turning her into as great a beauty as she had been as a bride. The elegant dress had a short skirt that showed off her well-shaped legs, and the expert make-up made her look delightful, the lavish hairstyle enhanced her. But when she offered to pay Naomi waved her away.

'That's all been taken care of,' she said.

'But can't I give you a tip to thank you?'

'That's been taken care of too. Mr Falcon was very insistent.'

'You mean he told you not to take a penny from me?'

Naomi smiled and shrugged. 'Mr Falcon is a very generous man.'

She hurried out.

Yes, he is, Freya thought. More than I ever knew.

Jackson was home at six o'clock, nodded approval at the sight of her, then disappeared to don his evening clothes. When he emerged she too nodded her approval.

'We'll do each other credit,' she said.

'That's the spirit. We'll show 'em.'

Downstairs, he loaded her case into his car and headed out onto the road.

'Where are we going?' she asked.

He gave her the name of a restaurant, famous for its glamour and luxury and for being a favourite home of major personalities. Within a few minutes they had arrived.

'Ready?' he asked as they headed for the entrance.

'Ready for anything,' she replied.

'Then here we go. Smile. They'll be watching.'

'Do they know we're coming?'

'I have a few friends in the press.'

Sure enough, heads turned as they entered. There were some cheerful waves, which Jackson returned.

A waiter showed them to a table, and the first

few moments were taken up with formalities. At last they were alone.

'Now, let's get down to business,' he said.

'Business?'

'You see those two over there?' he asked, nodding in the direction of a table where a young couple were holding hands and gazing rapturously into each other's eyes.

'Yes. But we're not going to do that, are we?' she asked, aghast.

'No way. Hell will freeze over before I ask you to give me *that* adoring look. They're an example of what we mustn't do. If we act like a couple in love it'll cause a scandal. People will think you were betraying Dan and that's why he headed for the hills.'

'Right. So what *do* we do?'

'We laugh. Let everyone see how light-hearted you are.'

'You've got this all worked out to the last detail, haven't you?'

'Is that a polite way of saying that I'm taking charge too precisely?'

'No, but you do seem to have a gift for organising. Perhaps nature meant you to be a film director.'

Jackson grinned. 'You're not the first person to say that, but the guy who said it first was really mad at me. He was the director of a TV show and I annoyed him by arguing all the time. "Everything's got to be done the way you say, hasn't it?" he yelled.'

'And what did you reply? *I'm glad you've realised that*?'

'You understand me far too well.'

Then the humour died from his face and he took a long breath.

'I went to see Dan today. There were a few sharp words and now I don't work for him any more.'

'Oh, no! Your career—I never meant to harm you.'

'You haven't. I was already thinking of leaving. Someone else has been in touch.'

He named a firm, high ranking in the production business.

'They've been dangling offers in front of me for a while. I didn't accept because I was OK where I was, but that's over now, so I called the man who runs this other place. He wants to do a series about ancient Egypt—myths, traditions, rituals, pyramids, that sort of thing. Once we've settled my contract I'll go out there to explore. It's a place that's always fascinated me.'

'Yes, it's got a magical reputation hasn't it? Tell me more.'

As Jackson talked she did as he'd suggested—smiling, nodding, seeming fascinated. Nobody must guess that inside she felt wretched.

She managed the pretence until Jackson finished by saying, 'So now we can both consign Dan to the past.'

She had a feeling of being punched in the stomach.

'Yes, we can, can't we?' she said bleakly.

'But I guess it won't happen all in a moment.' He looked intensely at her face. 'Perhaps I shouldn't have mentioned him.'

'No, I'm strong. I can cope.'

'I don't think you're as strong as you like to believe you are.'

'You're wrong,' she said firmly.

'I hope so. You'll get over him, Freya. You must.'

'Yes, I must,' she whispered, dismayed at hearing her voice crack on the last word. At all costs she must not weep.

Jackson took a gentle hold of her hand.

'You can't believe it now, but truly it will happen. The best of your life is still in front of you.'

'Yes—of course—it's just—I can't—' The tears were there again, refusing to be defeated.

'Come on,' Jackson said. 'Let's get out of here.'

He summoned the waiter, paid the bill and led her outside. She sat in silence on the journey. The courage and defiance that had carried her through the evening had vanished without warning, and she felt crushed.

When they reached the hotel he said, 'Shall I call your mother and tell her you're here?'

'No,' she whispered. 'I don't want to see anyone.'

'All right.' He kept his arm around her shoulders as they went up to her room, and went inside with her.

'Goodnight,' she said.

'Not yet. I don't like leaving you alone. You've been brave, and coped wonderfully, but nobody can be brave for ever.'

'They can if they have to,' she said huskily.

'But you don't have to. You've got a friend who'll always be there for you.'

'Don't,' she begged. 'I can manage—truly I can. I just need to—to—'

She tried to fight back the tears but it was hopeless. Grief devastated her.

'You need to do this,' Jackson said, taking her in his arms and drawing her close.

At once she gave up the fight for control. The warmth and sweetness of his gesture overcame her resistance and she let her head rest on his shoulder. He was right. While he was here she didn't need to be brave.

He turned his head, resting his cheek against her hair.

'Go on,' he murmured. 'Let it happen.'

She had no choice but to let it happen. Strong, controlled Freya could do nothing but yield to the despair she'd once managed to hold at bay. She could feel Jackson patting her shoulders as they shook with sobs, and for several minutes they stood quietly, leaning against each other.

She had the sensation of being in another world. It was warm, kindly, safe. She wanted to stay there for ever.

'Freya—'

His gentle voice made her look up to see his face just above hers, so close that she could feel his breath.

'Freya—' he murmured again.

There was something in his voice that she'd never heard before: uncertainty, perhaps even alarm.

'Freya—'

'Yes—'

She felt the touch of his lips against hers and drew in a soft breath. Next moment she was pressing against him, not even knowing what she did. Something deep inside her drove her on, telling her this was where she belonged. Without realising what she was doing she slipped her arms about him. She would have tightened them, but he tensed and raised his mouth from hers.

Suddenly tremors went through her body. The world had changed. She didn't know where she was. She knew only that this wasn't where she should be.

'Freya—'

'Let me go.'

The words were needless. He was already stepping back, putting distance between them.

'I'm sorry,' he said harshly. 'I didn't mean—'

'Neither did I,' she said, in a voice whose harshness matched his own. 'Please go now.'

'Freya, my dear—'

'I'm not your dear. I'm not your anything. Just because Dan dumped me, did you think I was there for the taking?'

'Of course not. I wasn't trying to make love to you. I promise that's one thing I'll never do. You can count on that. It was meant as comfort.'

'That's one kind of comfort I don't need.'

He seemed about to say something, but then his shoulders sagged as though he realised it was useless and he turned to the door.

'I'm sorry,' he said. 'It's not what you think. Don't be angry. I only wanted to help you.'

'Not like that,' she snapped. 'Goodbye, Jackson.'

He gave her an uneasy look, then left without another word.

He left her standing alone in the middle of the room, until her legs gave way and she collapsed onto the floor, wrapping her arms about her head, burying her face as though trying to hide from herself.

How could that have happened? How could she have felt that flickering of treacherous desire for Jackson when she was still dead inside from Dan's betrayal? She'd been so sure that all feeling was over for her, yet in a moment the old attraction for Jackson had come flickering out of the shadows, confusing, threatening.

'No,' she muttered. 'No, no, *no!*'

She'd run into his arms, grateful for the safety he'd seemed to offer. But there was no safety— only more devastation. The only safety lay in escape. She must get far away from him.

Monte Carlo. Janine and Amos would be leaving soon and she would go with them. Once there, she could retreat into herself and cease to exist as far as Jackson was concerned.

Cease to exist. It had a reassuring sound. And it was the only refuge that would not betray her.

She lay down on the bed and stared into the darkness for the rest of the night. Even darkness was reassuring now.

The next morning Freya went to Janine's and

Amos's room, glad to find her mother alone. Janine was delighted with her daughter's decision.

'You're coming with us? That's wonderful. If only we could convince Jackson to come too. He was here an hour ago and Amos was hoping to persuade him, but no luck. Such a pity.'

'He's starting a new job,' Freya said.

'So he said, but Amos is furious. They've had a big row. He's as stubborn as his father, so it's stalemate for the moment. But perhaps Jackson will change his mind and join us soon.'

'No,' Freya said quietly. 'I don't think he will.'

For Jackson to join them was the last thing she wanted. Nothing mattered now but to get a safe distance from him until she could cope with what had happened.

The next few days passed in a daze: the flight to Monte Carlo, the drive to Amos's magnificent house overlooking the bay, the feeling of having put trouble behind her at least for the moment.

Jackson stayed in touch, linking up via a video connection every evening, talking cheerfully to them from the screen. At first Freya watched these occasions from the sidelines, out of Jackson's sight, not joining in the conversations.

But then he noticed her before she could slip away and cried, 'Hey, there's my little sister. How's it going, sis?'

His use of the word 'sister' sounded like a message. He was telling her that their old pleasant relationship could be restored. But she doubted that could ever happen.

'It's going well,' she said.

'Glad to hear it.'

'Is everything all right with you?' she asked politely.

'I've never had such a fascinating trip. And, Dad, when I see you I've got something to tell you that'll really make you sit up…'

At last Jackson arrived at the villa. His greeting to Freya was friendly, without any tense edge. She knew a moment's resentment that he'd brushed everything aside so easily. Clearly what had happened mattered little to him and he thought it was the same with her. Yet he was right, she realised. Casual indifference was the only thing that would make each other's presence bearable.

Over a pleasant dinner Jackson told vivid tales.

'I've never regarded myself as a man suscep-tible to magic,' he said, 'but the magic began as soon as I arrived. I was in a hotel that looked out over the desert where the great pyramids are, and I could see one from my widow. I'll never forget standing there as dawn broke, seeing the pyra-mid slowly emerge from the darkness. And ev-erywhere I went—the temples, the Valley of the Kings—there was something that would make me stare with amazement.'

'But what was it you had to tell your father?' Janine said. 'We're dying of curiosity.'

'All right. Here goes. I had to study the Egyp-tian gods. There are many of them, with vary-ing degrees of power. One of the most powerful is called Horus.'

'But why should I be interested in him?' Amos wanted to know.

'Because he's known as the Falcon god. I couldn't believe it when I first heard that, but in pictures and statues he's represented as a falcon. Look.'

He reached into a bag and brought out a small statue of a bird with a cap on its head.

'That's Horus the Falcon god,' he said, handing it to Amos.

Janine burst out laughing at the sight of Amos's face as he studied the figure.

'You said it was powerful,' he murmured.

'He's the god of the sky, the sun and the moon,' Jackson explained. 'I thought you'd enjoy that.'

It was rare for Amos to smile with genuine pleasure, but now he managed a grin.

'That sounds about right,' he said.

'They knew about you all the time,' Freya teased him.

As the meal ended Jackson drew his father aside to tell him more colourful stories about Egypt.

'I'm so glad about that,' Janine told her daughter when they were alone. 'Amos is really enjoying it.'

'I wonder how powerful Horus really was,' Freya mused. 'Maybe Jackson has exaggerated a bit to please Amos.'

'Well, good for him if he has,' her mother said. 'It was nice.'

'Yes. He *is* nice, isn't he?'

The reminder of Jackson's kindly side gave

Freya a feeling of relief. At last she bade them all goodnight and went to bed. There she lay, brooding, wistful, daring to hope that perhaps the wretched memory could be banished into the shadows and their friendship could be restored. At last she fell asleep.

She was awoken by sounds coming from the next room, which she knew to be Jackson's. He was talking in a sharp voice, as though annoyed. The other man's voice sounded like Dan.

Rising quickly, she slipped on a dressing gown and went out into the corridor. Jackson's door was closed but she could hear the angry voices clearly.

'You should be ashamed of what you did,' Jackson snapped. 'And you damned well know it. Running off like that just before the wedding.'

'Don't heap all the blame on me,' came Dan's voice. 'You were the one who made it happen.'

'That's not true.'

'Yes, it is. You said it would be better to dump her then rather than later and I took your advice.'

For a moment Freya froze, then she flung open the door.

Jackson was sitting at his computer, confronting Dan, who glared back at him from the screen via a video link. Dan's face had a self-satisfied expression that she realised she had seen many times before. But it faded as he saw her come to stand behind Jackson. Just for a moment he was taken aback.

'Surprised to see me, Dan?' she asked coolly. 'After all the times you've avoided me it must come as a nasty shock.'

Jackson had also received a shock, going by his face as he looked up at her.

'Freya,' he said, almost stammering in his dismay, 'it's best if we talk later.'

'I'll talk to *you* later. I'll talk to him now.'

'There's not much to talk about,' Dan said.

'What did you mean about taking Jackson's advice?'

'I told him I wasn't keen on our marriage and he said I should dump you right away. I thought he knew best, so I did. I've got to go now, Freya. Goodbye.'

There was a click and Dan vanished from the screen.

Freya clutched her forehead.

'He's lying, isn't he?' she choked. 'Tell me he's lying. You never said anything like that.'

'He's twisted my words,' Jackson said desperately. 'He said he hadn't ever wanted to get married. He proposed because Amos tried to scare him off, not because of love. I was appalled that he'd deceived you and let it get so far. I said he should have been honest with you from the start, that he would hurt you more if he married you without love and let you down later.'

'So you *did* say it?' she demanded, aghast.

'Not the way he made it sound. I meant that he should never have planned a wedding in the first place, not that he should back off at the last minute. But he seized on it as a way out. Don't you see? It gave him an excuse to shift the blame. All right, I was clumsy and stupid, but not malicious. Please, Freya, try to understand. I never intended it to happen the way it did.'

'What do you mean about him proposing because of Amos?'

'Oh, heavens!' He groaned. 'Amos tried to make him back off, threatened him. Dan lost his temper and—'

'And that's why he proposed to me?' she whispered. 'That's all it was?'

'Yes.'

'He never loved me at all?'

'I'm afraid not.'

'And you've known this all the time?'

'I only found out on the way to the church. If I'd known earlier I'd have warned you, but it was too late.'

'Too late to warn me, but not too late to make him run for it.'

'I told you I never meant that to happen. I spoke clumsily.'

'You've deceived me—'

'No!'

'I begged you to tell me why he ran, but you never told me the truth—'

'I was as honest as I could be, but I couldn't repeat all the things he said. Have you forgotten the terrible state you were in that day? There was no way I could tell you everything. It would have finished you off, Freya. Please be fair.'

But she was too distraught to be fair.

'I trusted you,' she choked. 'Talked to you, told you things I'd never have told anyone else. And all the time you were laughing up your sleeve at me.'

'That isn't true. I was trying to do my best for

you. I'm sorry if I got it wrong, but I meant well. Call me an idiot, if you like, but don't call me a deceiver.'

'I believed you,' she whispered. 'Relied on you. I thought you were being so kind to me.'

'I felt terrible about what happened—how I helped to bring it about. I'd have done anything to make it up to you.'

'Anything except tell me the truth. Be honest, Jackson, if you know how. You've been enjoying watching me be an idiot, haven't you?'

'No, I swear it. Freya. you've got to believe me.'

'How can I? When I think of some of the things I said—how I trusted and confided in you. What a fool I must have sounded!'

'No, I was the fool for damaging you so idiotically. But I did my best to help you survive it—all right, it was a poor best, but I tried. Why don't we talk later, when you've had a chance to calm down?'

She had a feeling that a chilly bleakness had settled over the world.

'You think I'll see sense, don't you?' she said bitterly. 'You're wrong. Nothing will change. You won't ever look different to me from the way you do now. Mean, spiteful, contemptible.'

'Freya—' He reached out for her hand but she snatched it away.

'No, don't touch me. I can't bear the sight of you.'

'Please don't let this spoil our friendship.'

'There never was a friendship,' she whispered. 'There never could be.'

'Freya—'

He reached out for her again but she darted away. After a moment he heard her bedroom door shut and the key turn in the lock.

CHAPTER FOUR

ALONE IN HER room Freya slammed her fist down on the dressing table again and again. A storm had invaded her. Rage, bitterness, disillusion and misery fought for supremacy. They all won. She was trapped in their prison and inside her there was no escape.

But outside she could put distance between herself and Jackson. She hurriedly dressed, slipped quietly into the corridor, down the stairs and out of the door. She had no idea where she was going, except that a million miles away from him would not be far enough.

Once before the world had turned upside down, and she'd survived because of Jackson's comfort and support. But that had been only an illusion. Instead there was a bleak, arid desert where the rest of her life must be lived.

She lost track of time but she must have walked

for hours, because when she finally turned back the dawn was breaking.

Nearing the house, she saw her mother, standing at a downstairs window. As soon as she saw Freya she came to the front door.

'Come along in,' she said. 'I saw you leave. You were running as though the fiends of hell were after you. I was worried.'

'Sorry, Mum. That was inconsiderate of me, but I was ready to murder someone.'

'Ah, yes, Jackson got Dan on a video link, didn't he? I heard his voice. You still want to murder Dan?'

'No, Jackson,' Freya growled.

'What? Did I hear that right? But Jackson's been so nice to you.'

'Jackson is a lying, scheming, deceitful louse. And, yes, you heard that right. I said it and I mean it.'

'But he can't possibly have done anything to justify that. He's a fine, decent young man.'

'I thought so too. That's why I never realised what he'd really done.'

'Whatever do you mean?'

'It was because of him that Dan ran for it. He

never wanted to marry me, and when they were heading for the church Jackson urged him to dump me then rather than later. So Dan got out of the car.'

'Darling, I don't believe this. Jackson would never do such a thing.'

'He as good as admitted it. He says it was a mistake, but he doesn't deny Dan left me because of what he said.'

'Maybe that's why he's been so kind and helpful to you since then.'

'Don't try to defend him,' Freya flashed. 'He's deceived me.'

'But I don't understand. Why did Dan propose if he didn't want to marry you?'

'Because Amos forced his hand,' Freya said bitterly.

'Never! He was against that wedding. There's no way he ordered Dan to marry you.'

'Of course not. He ordered him *not* to marry me. Dan proposed just to show Amos that he couldn't be bullied. Then he regretted it, but he couldn't find a way out. When he and Jackson were in the car Dan told Jackson what had happened, and my brilliantly stupid stepbrother said the one thing that could make it worse. Dan seized his chance and vanished.'

'Amos *ordered* Dan to keep his distance from you? Surely not.'

'Why do you say that? Isn't it typical of Amos?'

'Darling, I've got no illusions about him. He goes through life doing what he wants. But he's too shrewd to do something so pathetically stupid. And he does have a nicer side. He's always been fond of you and he wanted to take you into the family—'

'No, it's more like claiming property. He doesn't have a daughter of his own, and he wanted me to "complete the set", because he can't bear not to have everything other people have. He didn't care which one of his sons he tied me to as long as he put his brand on me. When only Jackson was left he went mad because neither of us would give in.'

'This is terrible.' Janine groaned. 'But if Dan really only proposed for such a reason he'd have been a terrible husband. Jackson was stupid, but maybe he did you a favour in the long run.'

'Don't you dare stand up for him!' Freya cried. 'When I think of these last few weeks, how I've trusted and relied on him, and all the time he was hiding the truth.'

'Because the truth would have hurt you even more. How could he do that to you?'

'How could he have let me make such a fool of myself?'

'He probably wasn't thinking straight,' Janine said wryly. 'Men tend to do what they imagine will sort the problem today without realising that it might make it worse long-term. It obviously didn't occur to Amos that his threats would have exactly the opposite effect to the one he wanted.'

'I often wonder why you put up with him. Don't tell me it's for the money.'

'No, if anything his money has been a disadvantage. It looms so large in his life that it leaves no room for anything else.'

'Then why do you stay with him?'

'He needs me, my dear. He's vulnerable in ways he doesn't realise.'

'He'd never admit that.'

'No, he likes to see himself as powerful. That falcon god that Jackson brought back from Egypt has really sent him onto cloud nine. The trouble is, that's the side of him I find hardest to live with.'

'Does he know that? No, of course not. It would never occur to him that he doesn't come up to standard. I'd like to see his face when you tell him that you know what he did to Dan.'

'I'm not sure that I will tell him. And please don't you say anything.'

'All right, I'll leave it to you. How you handle your horrible husband is your affair.'

'Forget about Amos. This isn't about him. It's about Jackson. Don't condemn him too much for keeping quiet. He did it because he was feeling his way forward, moment by moment. He didn't ask himself what would happen when you found out later.'

'He never meant me to find out at all. He wanted to rule the roost all the time—just like Amos. Like father, like son. Haven't you noticed how alike they are? You don't see it at first, because Jackson can seem so charming, but every now and then you'll catch an expression on his face that makes him the image of Amos.'

'That's true,' Janine mused. 'I remember Dan telling us that producers were always getting annoyed because Jackson kept insisting that his way was best. He said it laughingly, but—yes, I can imagine.'

'So can I,' Freya said cynically. 'I don't think it ever crosses Jackson's mind that he might be wrong.'

Janine stared. 'Darling, what's got into you? You're even more upset than you were when Dan betrayed you.'

'I'm not upset, I'm furious,' Freya said quickly.

'It's more than that. This has hit you hard— even harder than Dan.'

'No! Of course it hasn't—it's just different. Please, I don't want to talk about it any more. And I think it's time I went back to London, got another job and made a new start.'

She didn't say that she wanted to delete Jackson from her life, but no words were necessary. Each knew what the other was thinking. They hugged, and then Freya left the room to head upstairs.

Neither of them saw the man standing back in the shadows, where he'd hastily retreated to avoid being discovered. Amos knew he needed time to consider everything that he'd overheard. And that perhaps all the time in the world would not be enough.

* * *

There was a flight to London later that morning and Freya secured a seat. When she appeared for breakfast she was already dressed to depart. She found Jackson at the table alone.

'We need a nice long talk,' he said to her in a low voice.

'I'm afraid not. I'm leaving in an hour.'

'What? Freya, you can't leave things like this. We have to sort it out.'

'There's nothing to sort. I've seen the truth about you now, and I don't like it. This is where it ends. You should be glad. I won't be a nuisance to you any more.'

He turned away and strode around the room, tearing at his hair.

'No, I'm not accepting this,' he said, returning to stand before her.

'I don't care what you accept. I didn't ask your permission,' she said furiously. 'I'm returning to London and I don't want to see or talk to you again.'

'You'd do this because I made one little mistake?'

'You treated me with contempt and I don't see that as a "little mistake".'

'Why must you be so unforgiving?' he demanded. 'I was wrong, I've admitted that. Now I want to put things right.'

'But they can't be put right. Ever. And that's final.'

Jackson stared at her as though seeing her for the first time. Or as though someone else had appeared in her place.

'I can't believe this is really you,' he breathed. 'I've never known you like this before—so hard and unforgiving.'

'I'm not hard. I'm just someone who's been pushed around and manipulated enough and I'm not going to put up with it any more. You think this isn't really me? It's the me I am now. She's different to the old one. Don't mess with her.'

Jackson met her eyes, trying to look deep inside and rediscover the woman he knew. But she'd vanished into thin air, leaving behind an enemy. There was a stab of pain in his heart, but at the same time his temper began to rise.

'Right,' he said. 'Then I won't mess with her. She's cold-hearted, ill-natured—well, never mind the rest.'

'Cold-hearted?' she echoed in fury. 'You *dare*

call me cold-hearted after everything that's happened? I'm the one who's been knocked down and kicked around by people I trusted. But perhaps you're right. It's time I became cold so that it can never happen again.'

'And you think you can protect yourself from pain for ever?'

'Yes, because people who feel nothing can't be hurt.'

'That's the coward's way out. I never thought I'd see it in you, but if you can't find it in your heart to forgive a mistake from someone who's truly sorry then you're not the woman I thought you were. Just who you are is something I won't stick around to find out. But I'll say this. Heaven help anyone you meet in future. Heaven help the man who's fool enough to fall in love with you. Because you'll kick him in the guts the first time he gets muddled.'

'That's all you think it was? A muddle? Oh, no! You just thought you knew better than anyone else.'

'Yes, I believed I was doing the right thing,' he shouted. 'Is that a crime?'

'It can be.'

'You're saying I was wrong to try to protect you from more pain? I failed, but I still think I was right to try.'

How like Amos he looked, with his face set and unrelenting.

'You're so sure you know best,' she challenged.

'That's why people do things. Because they think it's right at the time.'

'But some people *always* think they're right. Look, we're never going to agree. Let's leave it there.'

'Freya, why are you so determined to think the worst of me?'

'I don't have any choice.'

'Of course you do. Something's making you attack me far more than I deserve.'

'I've just reached a turning point, that's all. You said it yourself—there's another side of me coming out.'

'Then banish her fast, or she'll haunt you for ever.'

'Good. She'll keep me safe.'

'She'll destroy you.'

'That's my decision. And this time I know best. So let's get that clear and draw a line under it.'

His face grew even more tense, and she thought he was about to say something else, but the sound of Janine's voice outside startled them both and made them turn away from each other.

'There you are,' she said, entering the room. 'Have you seen Amos?'

'He's out there,' Jackson said, pointing through the window to where Amos could be seen sitting in the garden, staring out over the bay.

He was very still, unlike his normal restless self. They all watched him for a few moments, but he didn't move.

'It's time I was going to the airport,' Freya said. 'Perhaps Jackson could take you.'

'No!'

They both said it, speaking so swiftly and sharply that Janine was silenced.

Freya slipped away to collect her bags and went to wait in the garden. Amos was still there, still with his eyes fixed on the sea. Before approaching him she stood back, seeing him in a new, hostile light.

This was the man whose bullying had caused Dan's proposal, thus sowing the seed for the disaster that had followed. This was the man who had made Jackson what he was.

Slowly she approached him.

'I'm going back to England this morning,' she said.

'I hope you have a good journey. Is my chauffeur taking you to the airport?'

'No, I've called a taxi,' she said. She had no wish to accept favours from him. 'I'll say goodbye now.'

Reluctantly, it seemed to her, he turned his head to look up at her. But there was nothing in his eyes. They were as empty as a desert.

'Goodbye,' he said.

'Goodbye.'

When the taxi arrived mother and daughter hugged each other.

'Goodbye, Mum, I'll call you when I get home.'

'Goodbye, Freya,' Jackson said.

'Goodbye, Jackson.'

There was no hug between them. They exchanged brief nods, not letting their eyes meet. Both understood that this was goodbye in more than words.

As the taxi pulled away she didn't look back.

From now on Jackson would be out of her life and out of her mind. But still he haunted her on the flight back to London. Their last terrible quarrel thrummed inside her head, throwing up questions and possible answers.

He'd asked why she was so determined to think the worst of him. It was because she'd once thought the best, and now, from somewhere deep inside her, a protective armour was forming. It would prevent her from ever thinking the best of him again. And that was good. It would save her from a lot of pain.

On that she was resolved.

She would have to reorganise her life in more ways than one, since she had no job and nowhere to live.

As soon as she landed in London she checked into an airport hotel and called her mother.

'Are you all right?' Janine asked anxiously.

'I'm fine. Tomorrow I'm going to sign on with that private nursing agency I worked for once before.'

'The one that sends you to nurse people in their homes?'

'That's right. Then I'll solve my accommodation problem as well—at least until I've made some long-term plans. What's the atmosphere like there?'

'Very strange. Amos wants Jackson to tell him more about this falcon god, but Jackson says he hasn't time to talk. He's given him a list of websites, so Amos is glued to the computer. If I go into the room he finds an excuse to make me leave.'

'I guess he thinks he really is a god,' Freya said wryly.

'I'm afraid you may be right.'

'The best of luck in dealing with him. Bye.'

She ate alone in her room, then had an early night. Sleep came easily, but even there the questions clamoured. The bitter pain of discovering that Jackson wasn't the man she'd thought. The feeling that suddenly nothing in the world was safe, or would ever be safe again. Nothing would drive these away.

He was there in her dreams, regarding her with harsh, angry eyes, uttering cruel words. *Cold-hearted. Ill-natured.* He had actually called her those terrible names.

She gave a cry and awoke suddenly to find that tears were streaming down her face.

The next day she registered with the nursing agency, which immediately found her an assignment in London. She told herself that this was the start of a new life that would soon help her to forget the old one.

She often talked on the phone with Janine, who soon had startling news.

'You'll never guess what Amos has organised now,' she said. 'He's going to Egypt with Jackson.'

'Whatever for?'

'To play at being the falcon god, I suppose. He's even managed to get the production company on his side. They love Jackson being a Falcon, and now they've got two of them. So we can't stop him. Amos will be coming to London so that he can take the same flight as Jackson. I'll be coming too, to see him off.'

'Why don't you go to Egypt with him?'

'I would if I thought he wanted me. But things are very strange between us now. Sometimes I look up and catch him giving me an odd look.'

'What kind of odd look?'

'I can't describe it, but it's one I've never seen before. As though he wants to say something but isn't sure. I almost think he might be going to Egypt to escape from me.'

'That I don't believe. Not Amos.'

'But he's not the same Amos. He's a different Amos, and I don't know who. Now, darling, can we arrange to meet when we come to London?'

'Easily. My job's just finishing and I was about to ask for the next assignment.'

'Take a few days off and join us in the hotel so that we can have a little time together.'

Janine and Amos arrived two days later, and as soon as she met them she knew what her mother meant about Amos. It was as though a quietness had descended on him, making him totally unlike his usual self.

That night there were only the three of them at dinner. Jackson had called to say that there were last-minute affairs he must see to before he could leave the next day. Once again Freya felt herself dividing into two selves. One of them was disappointed not to see him; the other gave a sigh of relief.

She wondered if he too was relieved he could keep their meeting short, because next morning it was late when he joined them at the airport.

'Sorry,' he said, embracing Janine. 'Lost my passport at the last minute. All right now, though. Nice to see you, Freya. Right, Dad, are you ready to go? Good, then we'll be off. Goodbye, ladies.'

Janine opened her arms to her husband. He came into them, but only for a moment, and again Freya saw the sense of unease that he seemed to carry with him these days.

She was suddenly swamped by an irrational urge to hug Jackson. Despite the hostility that still burned between them it seemed unbearable to part as enemies. Disasters could happen. She might never see him again. Summoning all her courage, she took his arm and said, 'Don't I get a hug?'

His smile had a touch of wryness. 'Are you sure you want me to hug you?'

'I'll kick your shins if you don't,' she teased, trying to reintroduce some humour into their relationship.

'That's my girl,' he said, opening his arms.

His hug was brief, but fierce. 'Goodbye,' he said huskily.

'Goodbye. Jackson—'

'Gotta be going. Goodbye.'

Then it was over. The two men were walking away, and the two women watched their retreating figures with hearts that ached. At the entrance the men turned and waved one last time. Next moment they were gone.

Now Freya could really concentrate on putting her life back together. Dan was gone. Jackson was gone. She was free to make a new future.

She accepted another nursing assignment and when it was finished went out to Monte Carlo. In their phone calls something in her mother's manner had spoken of loneliness.

'Thank you for coming, darling,' she said fervently when Freya arrived. 'You can hold my hand and I can hold yours.'

Freya hugged her, but said, 'I don't need anyone to hold my hand. I'm managing just fine.'

Janine gave her a worried look, but was too wise to say anything.

'How are they doing in Egypt?' Freya asked over supper.

'Really well, apparently. Until now they've been in Giza, with the Great Pyramids and the Sphinx. But soon they're going to Edfu, where there's the temple of Horus. Amos is revelling in being a god.'

'Now, *there's* a surprise.'

The two women laughed.

'Jackson calls me sometimes, which I appreciate. It's kind of him to keep me in the picture.'

'Doesn't Amos keep you in the picture?'

'We talk, but I always feel that he's saying what he wants me to believe rather than telling me how things are.'

'And what he wants you to believe is that the world revolves around him—which, after all, is what he's used to.'

Janine gave a little sigh. 'Well, as long as it keeps him happy.'

'What about him keeping you happy? This is the twenty-first century. Men are supposed to worry about us as much as we worry about them.'

'I don't think many of them know that yet.

Jackson's kind and caring, but he's still an exception.'

'Yes, well let's not talk about that.'

'You're still upset with him? When I saw you hug him at the airport—'

'That was just a sentimental moment,' Freya said hastily. 'It came and it went. I've accepted reality.'

She spoke with a bright air that warned her mother to pursue it no further. Janine had hoped to find a softening in her daughter's attitude, but there was little to ease her mind.

'Freya, darling, can't you—? Oh, dear, there's somebody at the door.'

She rose and went out into the hall.

Left alone, Freya went to the window to look out at the glorious bay, where the sun was beginning to set. It was eight o'clock here, which meant that in Egypt it would be nine. What was it like as night fell on that mystical land? Was it as beautiful as daybreak?

She remembered Jackson saying, 'I'll never forget standing there as dawn broke, seeing the pyramid slowly emerge from the darkness.'

It was almost eerie the way he still haunted

her, cropping up at odd moments, forcing her to armour her mind against him.

The shrill of the telephone interrupted her thoughts.

'Can you answer that for me?' Janine called from the hall.

'All right.' She lifted the receiver. 'Hello?'

'Janine, thank goodness you're there,' said Jackson's voice.

'I—no. I'm—'

'I was afraid you might be out and I must talk to you urgently. I'm going to need your help, and I'll need Freya's help even more. It's Amos. He's started having breathless attacks and dizzy spells, but he won't admit there's anything wrong. I've told him he should go home, but he won't hear of it. He won't go to a doctor here either, so the only hope is for Freya to come to Egypt. He'll tolerate her keeping a daughterly eye on him.'

'Jackson—'

'And if Freya doesn't want to see me, tell her not to worry. I'll keep as clear of her as she pleases, just as long as she looks after Dad. That's all I'll ask of her. My word on it.'

Freya's head whirled. Since answering the

phone she'd uttered only a few words, and as her voice was very like her mother's Jackson hadn't spotted the mistake.

'Do you think she'll accept my word?' Jackson persisted. 'After what happened—does she still hate me?'

At last Freya forced herself to speak.

'I don't hate you, Jackson,' she said.

There was a stunned silence. At last he spoke, sounding shocked. 'Freya?'

'Yes, it's me. I'd have told you earlier but you didn't give me the chance. If you need my help you'll have it, of course.'

'Do you—mean that?'

'Of course I mean it. Ah, here's my mother. You'd better talk to her.'

She handed the phone to Janine, who had just appeared, murmuring, 'It's Jackson. He says Amos needs us.'

While Janine listened to the bad news Freya kept a comforting arm around her mother, supporting her when she seemed about to fall.

'Oh, no!' she wept. 'I'll come at once—'

'Me too,' Freya told her, taking the phone. 'Don't worry, Mum. I'm going to take care of everything.' Assuming her most professional voice, she said, 'Jackson, can you help me with the arrangements?'

'Certainly. We're at Giza, and the nearest airport is Cairo.'

For several minutes Freya made notes.

'As soon as I know the flight times I'll call you.'

'Fine. And, Freya, thank you for this. It means so much—I was afraid—'

'You should have known better. There's nothing I wouldn't do for my mother.'

'Oh, yes—of course. Right—'

He'd got the message. She was doing this for Janine, and only for her.

As soon as she'd replaced the receiver the two women fell into each other's arms.

'Thank you, darling,' her mother said in a choking voice. 'I don't know how I'd cope without you.'

'You don't have to,' Freya assured her. 'I'm here for you and I always will be. It's going to be all right. Trust me.'

'I do, darling. You're so strong. I think you can

do anything, fight any battle. As long as you're with me I know we're all safe.'

Freya smiled and said the right things, but inwardly she wished that she too could feel safe. She had no control over what would happen now, and the feeling of being helpless alarmed her. But she'd promised, and she was determined to help her suffering mother.

She would be strong to help her mother.

CHAPTER FIVE

THE NEAREST AIRPORT was close to the French town of Nice, about ten miles away. From there they could get a flight to Cairo. When the tickets were booked she called Jackson back.

'The first available seats are tomorrow afternoon. We'll land at—'

When she'd given him all the details he said, 'You'll be met there, and a car will take you to Giza.'

'Does Amos know we're coming?'

'Yes, but he thinks it's just a family visit because you're missing him.'

Freya went to help with the packing, concentrating everything on keeping her spirits up. She remembered asking Janine how she endured Amos, and her mother's answer: 'He needs me.'

That was love. Ignoring a man's displeasing ways to see only the vulnerability beneath was the very heart of love. And it was a feeling she'd never known with Dan, who'd never seemed vulnerable.

On the journey to Nice airport the next day Freya held Janine's hand, feeling that *she* was the mother now. The three hours of the flight seemed to stretch out interminably, filled with thoughts that she would rather avoid. As a distraction she buried herself in a book she'd bought about their destination.

She meant her physical destination. The other destination, the one gradually evolving inside herself, was a mystery as fathomless as ancient Egypt.

There were the pyramids, she thought, slowly turning the pages to see pictures of the great four-sided tombs that rose from huge bases to a high point.

The ancient pharaohs had ensured that the world would always remember them by creating extravagant burial temples, starting on the day they took the throne. The best known was Tutankhamun, the boy king who'd lived three and a half thousand years ago and died after a mere three-year reign aged only eighteen. His tomb was one of the smallest, but in the last century it had been excavated by explorers, and so made 'King Tut' the most famous pharaoh of them all.

Then there was the Sphinx, the huge statue of a lion with a human head, sometimes known as The Terrifying One.

Freya felt excitement growing in her at the thought of seeing this fascinating country.

At Cairo they went through the procedures of disembarking, collecting their luggage, going through Customs, searching the crowd.

'Who did he say he was sending to collect us?' Janine asked. 'Because I can't— *Amos!*'

She bounced up and down, waving frantically to someone. Now Freya recognised Amos, hurrying forward, gathering speed as he neared his wife until they flung themselves into each other's arms.

Freya searched the crowd for Jackson, but she could see no sign of him.

He wasn't there, she thought with a stab of disappointment. He hadn't bothered to come and meet them.

But then she saw him, standing a few feet away, looking so changed that she barely recognised him. The hot sun had tanned him, and he looked thinner, like a man who worked long hours and neglected himself. Despite the distance she could sense his tension, and she guessed he was really worried about his father and had taken a lot of trouble for him—even to the extent of seeking the help of a woman with whom he was at odds.

He looked up and she caught the exact moment when he saw her. New life came into his face and he raised a hand in greeting.

'Thank you,' he said as they met. 'It's wonderful that you're here. You can see how happy it makes Amos.'

The older couple were still hugging each other joyfully.

'I'm glad for both their sakes,' she said. 'And how are you? I nearly didn't recognise you.'

'It's been a little tiring, but I still love doing it.' He turned to his stepmother. 'Janine, lovely to see you.'

He enveloped her in a hug, then took their bags.

Freya had thought she too might have received a warm embrace from him, especially after the hug they'd shared when they parted. She thought perhaps she'd demanded that hug as a way of hinting that hostilities could now be over. She wasn't sure.

But things were different now. He'd promised to keep his distance and clearly he intended to do so. It was foolish to feel disappointed, and she wouldn't allow herself that much weakness.

Outside, a large, luxurious vehicle was awaiting them, with a chauffeur who took charge of their bags and assisted the ladies inside. With two rows of seats it was more like a bus than a car. Jackson guided the two women to sit together while he sat opposite, with his father.

'It should only take about half an hour,' he said. 'We're going to the Harbury Hotel in Pyramids Road.'

'Pyramids Road?' Janine echoed. 'Does that mean you can see pyramids from there?'

'I'll say it does,' Jackson agreed. 'You can hardly look in any direction without seeing pyramids. It's marvellous.'

They saw what he meant as soon as they reached the city. Tall buildings rose to the sky, but behind them, dominating the world, were the pointed shapes of the pyramids.

Soon they drew up outside the hotel—an immense, luxurious building. Porters took charge of their bags while Jackson escorted them to the desk to sign in.

'The whole television crew is staying here,' he said. 'They're out doing background shots at the moment, but they'll be here soon.'

Once upstairs, Amos showed Janine to his own room, which she would now share.

'Yours is just down here,' Jackson told Freya, leading the way. 'Next door to mine, so I'm on hand if you need help.'

The room was stunning, with a floor-to-ceiling window that opened out onto a balcony from which a huge pyramid could be seen. Holding her breath, Freya went out to stand there, trying to believe that so much beauty and magnificence was so close.

Turning back, she saw Jackson waiting patiently.

'Amos looks well,' she said. 'I hadn't expected to see him so vigorous.'

'He changes from moment to moment. Mostly he seems well, but then he'll go dizzy, or breathless. I make him rest when I can, but you know what it's like trying to get him to take advice.'

'You should know that better than anyone,' she pointed out. 'He's your father.'

'Yes, but I've never had to try to make him see sense before—not like this. You're the expert. If you knew what a relief it is to me to have you here.'

'You know I'll do my best to look after him.'

'That's very sweet and generous of you after everything that happened.'

'I'm not being sweet and generous,' she said at once. 'I'm being professional. Amos is my patient, even if he doesn't know it.' With a slight edge to her voice she said, 'Feelings have nothing to do with it.'

'Of course. I only meant— I don't want you to think— Well, anyway, I'm grateful.'

He stopped abruptly. The air seemed to ring with his confusion and suddenly she too was confused. It wasn't like Jackson to be lost for words.

'I'll leave you to get on with your unpacking,' he said at last. 'Tonight you'll meet the rest of the crew. It should be a cheerful party.'

'How have they felt about Amos being out here?'

'They love him. When he started talking about

the falcon god I saw Larry's face light up. That's Larry Lowton—the producer of the series. He's a terrific producer and he's treated Dad well. When we get to Edfu I think he's going to find a way of including him in the show.'

'What about you?'

'I'm always there, talking to the camera.'

'But you're a Falcon too. Doesn't he want to make use of that?'

'You're surely not suggesting that anyone could mistake *me* for a god, are you, Freya?'

'I suppose not.'

'Issuing edicts? Laying down the law? Nah! I'd be sure to make a mess of it, wouldn't I?' He regarded her with wry amusement. 'That's one thing I guess we can agree on.'

Here was dangerous territory. But she coped with ease, simply saying lightly, 'If you say so.'

'I do say so. Right, I'll be going now. I'll collect you in an hour.'

'How do you dress for dinner here?'

'Usually it's pretty casual, but not tonight. Everyone's poshing up in your honour. If you need me I'm just next door.'

He departed without waiting for a reply. Freya

gave a small sigh of relief. So far it hadn't gone too badly. Humour was a good way to deal with things.

It was a little disconcerting to know that he was next door, and when she went out onto the balcony she glanced at his window, ready to retreat if he appeared. But he didn't, and she was able to breathe in the magical atmosphere undisturbed.

She'd brought a couple of elegant cocktail dresses with her. For dinner she chose one in blue silk that fitted her figure neatly without too much emphasis. Like Jackson, she was keeping her distance.

There had been that troublesome moment at the airport, when she'd feared that he had not come. But her feelings were easily explained, she assured herself. They needed him as a guide. No more. Nothing about him could bother her now. Not even the fact that he was in the next room.

After an hour he presented himself, dressed in an evening jacket.

'You look fine,' he said politely. 'Let's go and collect our parents.'

Both Amos and Janine were smartly dressed for the evening, and Freya was glad to see that the atmosphere between them was warm. Amos seemed to be enjoying himself.

Seven people were waiting for them.

'This is Larry, the boss,' Jackson said lightly. 'He gives his orders and we all jump.'

'That's Jackson's idea of a joke,' Larry said. 'I don't think he's ever taken an order in his life.'

Freya took to Larry from the start. In his early forties, he was moderately handsome, if slightly on the plump side, and he seemed to live permanently on the edge of laughter. He introduced her to Tommy, his second-in-command, a lively, feverish young man who sent her an admiring message with his eyes and started blurting out incoherent words—which Larry firmly silenced.

'He's a good lad,' he told Freya under his breath, 'but he can be exhausting.'

Jackson joined them and introduced the rest of the team, finishing with a dazzlingly pretty young woman who greeted him with a peck on the cheek.

'This is Debra—Larry's excellent secretary,' Jackson explained. 'And sometimes she deigns to act as my secretary too.'

That wasn't her only role in his life, Freya

thought; not if her teasing manner towards him was anything to go by. She watched as he sat next to Debra, giving her his full attention, laughing at something she said, meeting her eyes.

When the introductions were finished Larry led Freya to a chair and pulled it out.

'Sit next to me,' he said. 'I want to know all about Jackson.'

'Surely you know plenty about him by now?' she said.

'Only the trivial things. But every time we argue he wins. That's got to stop. I want you to tell me about his weaknesses, so that I'll have him at a disadvantage instead of the other way around.'

He spoke in a loud voice, inviting everyone to share the joke.

Jackson grinned. 'He's been trying to catch me on the hop since the day we met,' he announced. 'No success so far.'

'But I can live in hope,' Larry declared. 'If this charming lady will be my co-conspirator?'

'Nothing would give me more pleasure,' Freya assured him. 'I could always tell you about the time three years ago when— Well, let's leave that until later.'

The mention of three years ago was a message to Jackson. This was a jokey conversation in which the recent past played no part. Tonight was simply for pleasure. His nod told her that he understood and agreed.

Larry was an entertaining companion, with a gift for telling anecdotes. One in particular reduced her to such a fit of laughter that everyone else at the table stared.

'I'm sorry,' she choked, bringing herself under control. 'It's the way you tell the story—were you ever an actor, by any chance?'

'Yes, I was,' he said. 'I started as an actor and gave it up to become a director. And you saw through me. Boy, you're really clever!' He took both her hands in his, gazing deeply into her eyes. 'Some time soon we must get together and you must tell me *all* about yourself.'

She wasn't fooled. This wasn't real flirting but a bit of harmless fun. And he expected her to understand it that way. His teasing glint made that clear. She had no problem in chuckling and saying with mock fervour, 'I can't wait.'

There was a cheer from the rest of the table, and cries of, 'Watch out for him, Freya. He's a dodgy character.'

'Well, I can see that,' she said. 'There's the fun.'

Tommy raised his glass, declaring, '*I'm* a dodgy character too. Don't forget me.'

'You'll have to wait,' she said. 'I only have time for one dodgy character at a time.'

The evening was a big success. Freya would gladly have stayed later, but she could see Amos trying to suppress a yawn and not succeeding. When Janine squeezed his hand he rose to follow her without protest.

'I'll come with you,' Freya said. 'Goodnight, everyone.'

'Goodnight,' Jackson said. 'Sleep well. We've got a heavy day tomorrow.'

Debra, sitting beside him, giggled and clutched his arm. Freya turned quickly away.

Upstairs, she and Janine worked at making Amos comfortable, to which he responded with the comment, 'Stop fussing, you two. I'm all right.'

'Of course you are,' Freya said. 'I'll see you in the morning.'

She kissed her mother and departed. Now she badly wanted to be alone and it was a relief to escape to her room. Once inside she didn't put on the light, but opened the glass door onto the balcony and went out into the night air.

A soft light still gleamed on the pyramids, making them glow faintly. Entranced, she stood watching, enjoying the feeling that she was witnessing a mystery that stretched back centuries. It was a sweet, magical feeling that seemed to take her back to another time, when the world itself had seemed imbued by magic.

But what folly that had been. And how quickly, how brutally it had ended.

She was swept by a strange mood; deep inside her there was a kind of anguish—not for Dan himself, but for what he had seemed to represent: hope, wonder, a belief that life could be beautiful.

For a while after the disaster of her wedding she'd been able to continue believing. Jackson had reached out to her, and while she'd been able to cling to him the world had still been a good place. The discovery of his betrayal had been a blow over the heart that had affected her as much as Dan's. Perhaps even more.

Now the comfort that Jackson had seemed to offer was gone. Gone for ever. For how could she ever believe in anyone again?

She dropped her head, covering her eyes with her hand, seeking escape, forgetfulness, while her body trembled with sobs.

'No,' she told herself sharply. 'I said I wasn't going to give in to this again. And I'm not. I'm going to have a new world that I'll build myself, without anyone's help.'

But somehow strength and resolution were no help to her now. She gazed yearningly at the pyramid, looming high and peaceful as it had done for thousands of years—as it would do for thousands more. How petty seemed human problems against that monument and the ancient wisdom it represented. How many humans had stood before its magnificence feeling their own triviality?

'If only I knew what I—' she whispered. 'If only I could tell—'

But there was only silence and the awesome, unyielding beauty that seemed to come from another universe.

At last she turned away and moved inside, where she went to bed and lay sleepless for several hours.

For several minutes after Freya went inside, the man standing on the next balcony stayed silent and motionless, relieved that she hadn't discovered him.

Jackson wasn't proud of himself for watching Freya while she hadn't known he was there, but her entrance had taken him by surprise. He remembered that day several weeks ago, when she'd discovered his innocent deception about Dan and attacked him furiously. A few hours later he'd spotted his father standing outside the door, secretly listening to Freya and her mother talking inside. Without being able to make out the words, Jackson had guessed what was being said.

Seeing his son, Amos had placed a finger over his lips and shaken his head. When Jackson had tried to make him leave he'd refused. Nor would he discuss what he'd heard.

'And don't you tell them that you saw me,' he'd demanded. 'There are things a man should keep to himself.'

Jackson had agreed, though reluctantly. Having concealed the truth from Freya once, it hurt him to deceive her by concealment a second time. It had been a relief to leave for Egypt soon afterwards. Now a malevolent fate had tricked him into spying on her. Leaving the balcony had been impossible. The door to his bedroom was too noisy to risk. He'd had no choice but to stay and see things his conscience told him he had no right to see.

Like father, like son, he thought bitterly. He always said he wasn't like Amos, but then something like this happened and—oh, hell!

The quarrel with Freya had hurt him. When he'd first tried to help her through the misery of her cancelled wedding it had been partly from kindness, partly from guilt. Gradually he'd come to enjoy their relationship. The sense that he could bring her comfort had made him feel good about himself in a way that had been new to him.

Which just went to show how conceited he could be, he told himself wryly.

The pleasure of protecting her had been real, and her fury when she'd discovered the truth had been a blow to his heart. Then she'd seen him off at the airport and demanded a hug, giving him a moment of hope. He'd dared to think next time they met the past would be forgiven, their friendship restored.

But then had come his call to England about Amos's health, and the things he'd said to Freya thinking he was speaking to Janine. He'd said nothing that could offend her, but he'd adopted a pleading tone that now embarrassed him. How foolish he must have sounded.

When they'd met again earlier that day she'd been coolly affable, full of calm good sense. No sign of hostility, but no pleasure either. It was as though the old, friendly Freya no longer existed.

But she'd returned tonight at the dinner table. Chatting with Larry, she'd burst into delighted laughter, then indulged in a bout of teasing back-chat with him.

Debra, sitting beside himself, trying to lure his attention away from Freya, had murmured, 'Those two are really on each other's wavelength, aren't they?'

'Are they?' he'd responded with a fairly convincing display of indifference.

'No doubt of it. He took to her from the first moment. You've got to admit she's a looker.'

'Is she?' Freya's personality had always appealed to him more than her looks. Studying her at that moment, he'd had to admit she was at her best—much as she had been on her wedding day.

'Oh, come on!' Debra had exclaimed. 'She's really pretty, but Larry likes them best when they laugh with him.'

'Would you like some more wine?' he'd asked with a fixed smile.

He would have offered her anything to shut her up.

Now there was no doubt. The Freya he'd once known hadn't disappeared after all. She was reappearing, as lively, jokey and fun-loving as always.

But for Larry. Not for himself.

He'd promised to keep his distance, and for his father's sake that promise had to be kept. So he'd given her only the attention that courtesy demanded. Then he'd hidden behind the shield Debra offered, flirting with her, seeming riveted by her company, to conceal the fact that his real attention was for Freya. He'd tried to be glad that she was getting on so well with Larry, but somehow he just hadn't been able to manage it.

When the meal was over he'd seen Debra to her door and bade her a courteous goodnight, pretending not to see the invitation in her eyes, or her bafflement when he ignored it. Then he'd returned to his own room.

There had been no light under Freya's door, suggesting that she hadn't returned. Where was she? he'd wondered. Alone? Or had her joke about dodgy characters being fun actually held some meaning? Was she exploring that meaning? With Larry?

No, not Freya. Not after one brief meeting.

Surely not.

But then where *was* she?

He'd gone out to look at the pyramid, looming in the darkness, and had still been standing there when she'd arrived next door. Straining his ears, he'd heard no voices and realised, with relief, that she was alone. Next moment she'd appeared on her balcony.

He'd moved forward, meaning to speak to her, then stopped. Something about her as she'd stood there, gazing up into the night, had made him pause, enjoying the air of rapture that seemed to permeate her being. But it had passed suddenly, replaced by a sigh.

He'd watched as her shoulders had sagged, hoping to see her pleasure return. Instead she'd dropped her head in her hands and he'd been able to hear her weeping.

He'd clenched his hands, longing to reveal himself and comfort her but knowing that he didn't dare. She would never forgive him.

He'd seen the sobs convulse her, possessing her whole body with a nameless grief. Frantically he had sought for the answer. Was it the sight of himself that had hurt her after so long? Or did the pain of that terrible day still torment her, reducing everything else to nothing?

In the aftermath of her wrecked wedding, how often had he heard her declare defiantly that she wasn't going to cry? She hadn't always managed to fight back the tears, but her courage and defiance had seldom faltered. He'd known her confident, efficient at her job, ready to confront life on equal terms. But until now he hadn't known her defeated.

The sight of her yielding to despair had made

him long to reach out and console her. It would have been easy to climb the low wall that separated his balcony from hers and take her in his arms, lavish her with warmth and comfort. For a moment he'd been fiercely tempted, knowing that only he could comfort her because only he knew the full extent of her hurt.

He had reached out his hand to the wall.

But then he'd stopped himself and drawn back in alarm. Once he could have consoled her as a brother, but those days were over. The physical attraction that had flickered between them might have been brief, but its memory was searing. Neither of them could forget it, and it would destroy everything he tried to do for her. Now she was alone as never before.

The sight of her tears had seemed to bring a treacherous stinging to his own eyes, and bitterly he'd cursed the malign fate that made him helpless when she needed him so much.

At last Freya had turned away and stumbled inside, leaving him distraught and asking himself for the thousandth time, *What have I done?*

CHAPTER SIX

THE RINGING OF the phone awoke Freya before dawn the next morning. It was Janine, sounding worried.

'Please come,' she said. 'He's gasping again.'

Freya pulled on her dressing gown and hurried out into the corridor. To her surprise she saw Jackson there, turning the key in his own door.

'What is it?' he asked.

'Amos. Mum's just called me to say he's gasping.'

'Let's go.'

They found Amos sitting on the side of the bed, his chest rising and falling heavily. He looked up at Freya, and nodded when she produced the stethoscope she'd taken the precaution of bringing.

'So now we have the truth,' he said caustically. 'Your visit is just another way of mollycoddling me.'

'I'm always ready in case you need me. Now hush and let me do my job.'

'Are you giving me orders?'

'Yes, I am. So do as I say and be quiet.'

'You're as big a bully as your mother.'

'Luckily for you I am.'

She listened to his heart, fearing the worst, but was pleasantly surprised to hear it beating strongly.

'That's good,' she said.

'Of course it is. There's nothing the matter with me. Why must women always make a fuss?'

'Because you mean a lot to us,' Janine said, sounding cross. 'Although I sometimes wonder why. You miserable old so-and-so.'

Amos gave a bark of ironic laughter. 'And those are the words of a woman who says I mean a lot to her. Isn't it lucky I have a sense of humour?'

'No, it's lucky you have a wife who can put up with your carry-on,' Freya said. 'Your health isn't too bad but don't overdo it.'

'If you're trying to stop me going out today, forget it. It's our last day here before we go to Edfu and I'm not going to miss it.'

'Perhaps you should,' Jackson said. 'You've

seen this place. Why not stay here and rest today so that you're fit for tomorrow?'

'I'm fit for anything I say I'm fit for,' Amos said, outraged. 'Don't tell me you've started taking their orders? That any son of mine—'

'As a son of yours I'm practical,' Jackson said. 'And being practical means I'll listen to suggestions from someone who knows better than I do.' He inclined his head to Freya. 'Find the experts and pick their brains. It's the most profitable way forward. You taught me that.'

'I'm going with you,' Amos repeated.

'All right, but take it easy,' Freya told him. 'Walk as little as you have to.' She had a sudden burst of inspiration. 'After all, our next stop is Edfu, where you and Horus will confront each other. You wouldn't want to be taken ill before you get there, would you? Imagine missing him when you've come so far to meet him. He's probably laying out the red carpet for you now.'

Amos cast her a wry look, conveying that he understood exactly what she was up to. But to their relief his mood improved.

'You're right,' he said. 'Nothing must get in the way of Edfu.'

'It's still early,' Freya said. 'Try to get some more sleep.'

Amos nodded and slid down in the bed. Jackson and Freya patted Janine's shoulder, and left.

'Is he really all right?' he asked as they went along the corridor.

'Yes, his heart sounds better than I expected. But he shouldn't walk too much. It might help to have a wheelchair on hand, just in case.'

'Gladly. You really got the better of him back there.'

'No, you did, with your talk about profiting from the advice of experts.' She put her hand over her mouth to smother a yawn.

'And you're the expert,' he said. 'You'd better get a little more sleep. You might find tomorrow tiring. Goodnight.'

'Goodnight.'

Where was he going? she wondered as he walked away. Back to Debra, perhaps.

She remembered hearing him spoken of as 'a man who likes to enjoy life, taking pleasure wherever he finds it', and she guessed the pleasures must be many. Women would be drawn to both his looks and his growing fame as a television personality. And his easygoing good nature would add to his attractions.

As for his darker side, the one that had ruined things between them, who else but her had ever discovered it?

She had no desire to sleep. She switched on the light and took out the book about the pyramids that she'd brought with her. But even this failed to calm her mind and at last she closed it, turned the light out again and went to the window that looked out over the hotel's garden.

In the faint light she could just make out the figure of a man wandering beneath the trees. Something about him caught her attention. He seemed not merely alone but strangely cut off from his fellow humans.

Then she recognised Jackson.

So he wasn't with Debra, she thought. Unless Debra was coming out to join him.

But minutes passed and he was still alone. Again she had the mysterious feeling that loneliness was natural to him.

How could that be? Nobody as popular as Jackson was ever lonely.

Yet the thought would not be banished. For all

his large family, his popularity, Jackson had no-body who was completely his. His brothers were all happily married; his father had Janine. But he drifted through life in mysterious isolation. The thought had never occurred to her before, and now she wondered why.

He turned, looked up and saw her. She half ex-pected him to turn away, but he raised his arm in a gesture that invited her to join him. Her heart leapt. She waved back, and hurried away to slip some shorts and a T-shirt on before going to meet Jackson.

He was waiting for her at the door.

'Thank you,' he said. 'I was afraid you wouldn't come.'

'But this is a lovely place. I don't wonder you like to be here.'

He took her hand and led her through the trees to where there were some seats at the end of the garden. The pyramids were more visible now, easing their way into the light, magical, mag-nificent, mysterious.

For a while they sat in silence, relishing the ex-perience, his hand still holding hers. Then he said softly, 'I can't tell you how grateful I am to you for coming to Egypt. It must have been difficult.'

'I wouldn't just abandon Amos. I know he means the world to you.'

'In a way.'

'In a *way*?'

'Don't misunderstand me. I love my father. But—how do I say it?—I don't always like him. He does what suits himself, no matter who he hurts.'

He paused and she had a vivid sense of indecision tormenting him. His words were heavy with a meaning he'd never hinted at before and perhaps couldn't speak of now.

'Is there anything you want to tell me?' she asked gently.

His hand tightened on hers.

'I've never talked about it before,' he said huskily. 'But now I— For the first few years of my life I seemed to be part of the ideal family. There were my parents, and Darius, my brother, and everything was fine. Then my mother found out about my brother Marcel—the son he'd had by Claire, a Frenchwoman, five years earlier.'

'While he was still living with your mother?'

'Yes. I think that was one of the things that hurt her most. That he'd carried on with another woman while still playing the loving husband.'

'How could she ever believe a word he said after that?' Freya breathed.

'She couldn't. She left him. They divorced and he married Claire. Darius and I lived with our mother until she died a few years later. After that we had to return to Amos.'

'How old were you then?'

'Eleven. I could never be at ease with Claire. It wasn't her fault. She was my father's victim as much as any of us. But I blamed her for my mother's death.'

'You don't mean your mother—?'

'No, she didn't take her life. Not exactly. But she went down with an illness that she didn't have the strength to fight, and I don't think she wanted to fight it. I was with her when she died, and the last thing she said to me was, "I'm sorry." Then she closed her eyes and just let go. Meanwhile Amos was playing the field again, with Travis's mother in Los Angeles and Leonid's mother in Moscow. Claire found out and left him, taking Marcel. By then Darius was making his own career, so I was alone with Dad for much of the time.

'It was like living with two versions of the same person. There was the man who'd broken all our hearts and didn't care—a man I resented. But there was also the "Big Beast", whom the world admired and feared, and in a way I admired him too. I wanted to be like him, earn his praise. I did some really stupid things, and the stupider I was the more he approved of me.'

'But approval wasn't enough, was it?' she asked.

'No. I wanted more. I wanted—I don't know—something else.'

'Love,' she said. 'The kind that puts you first—the kind you should expect from your parents. When grown-ups are so taken up with each other they can sometimes forget what the children need.'

He stared. 'How did you know that? Surely your parents loved you?'

'Oh, yes, but they loved each other first. I got lavish presents, but somehow I always sensed something missing. One year my father paid for me to go on a really expensive school trip. I thought he was being generous, finding so much money for me to enjoy myself. But while I was gone he and my mother took a holiday together. I thought there would be another holiday, with the three of us, but there wasn't. They'd seized the chance go away without me. I know it sounds crazy and self-centred to say it like this—'

'Not to me, it doesn't,' Jackson said. 'Everything's fine on the outside, but inside there's a place that's sad, hollow.'

As he said it she could see the child Jackson, surrounded by money and success but knowing there was no one who would put him first. The father playing the field with other women…the mother more concerned with her own misery than her children's needs.

'That's it,' she said. 'I grew up knowing that I'd have to be enough for myself. Or at least pretend to be.'

'Yes.' Jackson sighed. 'Exactly like that. It can be good to be enough for yourself, as long as you know when to drop the defences. That's Dad's trouble. He never knew. Through all those love affairs he had to be the one in control.'

They looked at each other, sharing the same curious expression.

'We've known each other for six years,' he said. 'And we've never shared this before.'

'It was never the right time before,' she said.

'Yes. And when the right time comes, you know. And you have to take it because it may never come again. I think you're the only person I could ever talk to about Dad, and how tense I feel about what I've inherited of his nature.'

'You can't help what you were born with. And you're not as bad as he is.'

'Thanks. I treasure that.' He added wryly, 'And a gift for getting your own way *can* be useful. But sometimes it makes me wonder about myself. I've got a bad side.'

'So have we all,' she said. 'Don't be hard on yourself.'

'That's nice of you, but my bad side is worse than you know. And you know plenty, after the harm I did you.'

'But you didn't do it on purpose. You made an incautious remark. You couldn't predict what Dan would do. It was a mistake, but I've made plenty of those myself. Let's draw a line under it.'

He stared. 'You've really forgiven me?'

'There's nothing to forgive. You might have been a bit clumsy—'

'Clumsy, stupid, idiotic, thoughtless—' he supplied.

'If you say so. But you weren't spiteful. You're not capable of spite.'

'That's kinder than I deserve.'

His voice was heavy and she knew he was still deeply troubled—not only by their past hostility but by the burdens Amos had loaded onto him when he was too young to bear them.

He dropped his head, fixing his gaze on the ground. She knew a deep and worrying instinct to protect him. Dazzling, self-confident Jackson had never seemed in need of anyone's protection before, but this was a new man—one he'd revealed to her and perhaps to nobody else. He trusted her. He'd said so, and had proved it by showing his vulnerable side.

In another moment she would have reached out and taken him in her arms, offering him all the comfort she could, but a warning sounded in her head. That way lay danger. The faint, flickering attraction between them might revive at any time.

The memory of his lips brushing hers warned her not to take the risk.

Yet who else was there to help him? His obnoxious father? The women who came and went but never seemed to get really close to his life or his heart?

She could have cursed the malign fate that had given such insight to *her*—the one person who didn't dare use it, and yet who wanted to use it with all her heart. It was alarming how much she wanted that.

She ventured to reach out and touch his shoulder.

'Jackson—'

He raised his head and their eyes met. For a brief moment she saw him defenceless, without the mask that she now realised he wore so easily.

'What is it, Freya?' he whispered.

She drew a trembling breath. Another moment and she would have thrown caution to the winds. But alarm came to her aid, forcing her to speak common sense words.

'Let's put it in the past,' she said. 'We've always been good friends and we're not going to let anything spoil it.'

'Right,' he said, and the mask was in place again. 'Good friends it is—just like always.'

'Always have been, always will be.'

They shook hands.

'Oh, look,' she said. 'It's there.'

The great pyramid loomed gloriously above them, golden in the fast growing light, full of promise for the day to come.

'Yes, it's there,' he said. 'It could be there for ever.'

'When we're not here any more—in a thousand years.'

They sat in silence for a while. At last they rose and wandered back into the hotel. It was time for the day to begin.

At breakfast Amos was in good spirits.

'I'm beginning to find Ancient Egypt fascinating,' Freya told him. 'This place we're going to today—'

'The Giza Necropolis,' Amos put in.

'Yes, the place with all those pyramids. Will I see Tutankhamun's tomb?'

'No, that's not here,' Amos said. 'He's further down the Nile, in the Valley of the Kings. But it's quite near Edfu, so you can see him when we go there.'

'So who *is* in the Giza Necropolis?' Freya asked.

'Khentkaus the First,' Amos said.

'Who was he?'

'Not he—she,' Jackson said. 'We don't know very much about her—even who she really was. There are a thousand stories that she was the daughter of one pharaoh and the wife of another—maybe two others. She might have reigned in her own right—or maybe not. Or perhaps she was the mother of two pharaohs and the regent of one. All we know for sure is that she must have been someone important for her tomb to be located here, among kings. Apart from that she's a woman of mystery.'

'I thought Cleopatra was the great woman of mystery,' Freya observed.

'In a sense,' Jackson agreed. 'But we know so much about Cleopatra that there's less mystery to enjoy. Khentkaus hides behind a fog of ambiguity.'

'Ah, yes, that sounds far more fun,' Freya agreed.

'Definitely.'

They shared a nod.

'Time we were going,' Larry said.

Of the journey out to the Giza Necropolis she gazed, entranced, out of the window.

'Where's Khentkaus?' she asked.

'Her pyramid is just a ruin,' Jackson said. 'There's very little to see. We'll do a final shoot today and bid her goodbye.'

No sooner had they arrived than Larry summoned Jackson, saying, 'We've got a problem.'

'He doesn't look pleased,' Freya observed, for Larry's face bore signs of intense exasperation. 'Have you offended him?'

'You bet I have,' Jackson said. 'I made some changes to the script we're shooting. I often do that, and it makes him mad.'

'I shouldn't think the scriptwriter's too pleased either.'

'No, but he's a wise man. He just keeps quiet and does what the boss tells him.'

'The boss being Larry?'

'Officially…'

'And unofficially?'

Jackson grinned. 'What do you think?'

'That's the spirit,' Amos declared, delighted.

'I guess I'm not your son for nothing,' Jackson said. 'But I sometimes have to make a show of deferring to Larry, just to keep the peace. From the way he's holding up that script and thumping it, this may be one of those times.'

He went over to Larry. The others watched, fascinated to see what would happen next, but they were disappointed when both men walked away and disappeared behind some stones.

'That's a pity,' Freya said. 'It could have been fun.'

'Jackson will win,' Debra predicted. 'He always does. He likes to change the words and even direct the research. And if he doesn't get what he wants there's trouble.'

'There they are,' Freya said, pointing.

Larry and Jackson had reappeared, still arguing. The listeners could make out most of the words.

'It's just that I can't see it that way,' Larry was saying. 'The original idea—'

'The original idea was full of holes, and it's got to be put right.' Jackson jabbed at something in the script. 'I can't say that. It doesn't make sense. I've told you what I'm going to say instead.'

'If you can get Pete to agree.'

Pete was the scriptwriter.

'No, *you'll* do that. Just tell him everything's been decided.'

'And has it?'

'You know it has.' Jackson's grin made him charming, although his words were implacable. 'C'mon, we've sorted it now. I'm not going to stand up before the camera and say something I don't agree with, so that's it. It's all settled.'

Jackson returned to their side.

'Larry's agreed to the script change. I had to admit I'd been in two minds about it at first—'

'That was bad,' Amos said quickly. 'You shouldn't have admitted that.'

'Well, it didn't do any harm. He's even going to arrange some extra shots to illustrate what I'm going to say.'

'Good. You did well. Mind you, you took too long. You should have been firmer from the start. Then he'd have capitulated sooner.'

'And there would have been a lot of bad feeling,' Jackson said. 'I work with these people. I don't want bad feeling. It's better my way.'

Amos shook his head.

'You still have something to learn about standing up to people. For one thing, you should never tell them anything they might use against you. Never let them suspect a weakness. But you'll learn. Wait till you reach my age.'

'I'm not sure I'll ever reach your age. Freya will have strangled me long before that. Right—time to get to work.'

Before leaving he gave Freya a significant look that she understood at once. He was reminding her of their talk in the dawn, of how troubled he was by this side of him although he couldn't help making use of it. She offered him a smile of reassurance and he gave her a brief nod.

Everything went well after that. Despite his firm stand Jackson still managed to stay on good terms with the others. She watched him with interest, fascinated by his expertise as he led the cameras over the ruins of Khentkaus' tomb and delivered a eulogy.

'After thousands of years,' he said, 'there are still many questions. How many of her children took the throne? How many of her descendants walk the world today? Truly she was a woman of mystery, and the mystery lingers even now. Will those questions ever be answered? Probably not. Like many a woman of mystery, she prefers to keep her secrets to herself.'

He gave the smile that had done so much to win him an audience of eager fans.

'But one day—who knows?—perhaps she will choose to open her heart to us.'

'Cut!' Larry yelled. 'That's great. All right, everyone. Time to go.'

Dinner that night was cheerful. Debra even made a jokey comment about the argument she and Freya had witnessed.

'You won, then?' she teased Jackson.

'Of course,' Jackson declared, raising his glass in Larry's direction.

'It's got something to do with him being a Falcon,' Larry said, 'and there being a falcon god. I had to make use of that.'

'I think it's a great idea,' Freya said.

'Of course. After all, your own name is an invitation all by itself.'

'My name?' she echoed, puzzled.

Larry regarded her quizzically. 'Don't say you don't know?'

'Know what?'

'That you're a goddess?'

'Oh, come on—'

'No—really. Freya comes from Norse mythology. She's associated with fertility and she rides a chariot pulled by two cats. You actually didn't know you're a goddess?'

'No, and I don't believe it. Mum—?' Freya turned to Janine. 'Surely not.'

'It's possible. Your father chose your name. He was fascinated by mythology, and he said he'd found it in a book, but that was all. It might be true.'

'There's another thing,' Larry said, clearly enjoying every moment. 'The great goddess Freya wears a cloak of falcon feathers, so in a way you're a falcon too.'

Amos gave a crack of laughter. 'How about that? You've been a Falcon all the time.'

'Hardly,' Freya said. 'I think it takes a bit more than wearing a cloak.'

'You'd better watch out, Dad,' Jackson said.

'You've met your match.' He raised his glass to Freya. 'I salute you.'

Amos immediately did the same, and everyone joined in.

'You should do a programme about her,' Amos asserted.

'And perhaps Khentkaus as well,' Larry agreed. 'I remember once hearing somebody say that the most interesting crimes were committed by women.'

More laughter—except from Freya, whose face grew suddenly darker. But nobody seemed to notice except perhaps Jackson, who became suddenly intent on clinking glasses with everyone near him. Except Freya.

When it was time to retire Freya accompanied Amos and Janine to their room and made sure Amos was comfortable. Returning to her own room, she went outside onto the balcony to take a last look at the pyramids glowing against the night.

'Are you all right?'

Jackson's voice, coming from a few feet away, startled her. She could just make him out on his own balcony, standing quietly in the darkness.

'I—I didn't know you were there,' she stammered.

'Sorry, I didn't mean to alarm you. I was just a little concerned in case you were upset. You went quiet very suddenly at dinner, and I think I knew why. It was what Larry said about women committing the most interesting crimes. I suddenly remembered Dan saying the same thing. It came out of a book he'd read.'

'Yes, he talked to me about it. It just reminded me of him. But it's nothing.'

'Nothing? It was like he'd suddenly appeared in front of you and you were shattered.'

'No, I wasn't. Just a little surprised. But he doesn't trouble me any more.'

'I'd be glad to believe that, but I worry about you.'

'Don't. Dan isn't part of my life any more.' She assumed a dramatic air. 'Freya the goddess waved her magic wand and he ceased to exist. That's how powerful she is.'

'If only life could be that simple. We all have things we'd like to wipe out as though they'd never happened, but the more we want to be rid of them the more they seem to haunt us.'

Freya shook her head firmly. 'I'm not haunted. I don't let that happen.'

'And Freya the goddess is in complete control, eh?'

'Yes. You'd be surprised how powerful she is.'

'I'm not sure that I really would be surprised. I think you keep a lot up your sleeve, Freya.'

'I do these days—now that I've discovered how much other people keep up their sleeves.'

'Was that aimed at me?'

'Not really. No, it was more aimed at Dan.'

'So he really is still there, isn't he? I wonder—'

'It's late,' she interrupted him. 'I think I'll go to bed. Goodnight, Jackson.'

'Goodnight, Freya. Sleep peacefully.'

But he knew that he himself would be denied peace that night.

After trying without success to fall asleep, he rose from his bed and switched on his computer. A few clicks and he had what he sought.

There she was, Freya the glorious goddess, a magnificent being who carried in her train not only fertility but also beauty, war and death. One artist's impression had managed to catch all those hints.

'You'd really have to be wary of *her*,' Jackson murmured aloud. 'Because there's so much more in her than you'd ever dream at first. And you'd know only what she chose to reveal.'

He stared intently at the face on the screen, wishing that it was another face and he could reach out to it.

'A true woman of mystery...' he said.

CHAPTER SEVEN

FROM GIZA TO Edfu it was nearly two hundred miles. Once the coaches had started their journey Freya spent much of the time studying a book on Horus that Amos had bought in the hotel.

One of the greatest deities of ancient Egypt, whose influence stretched over three thousand years...

He'd been born to the goddess Isis when she had rescued the dismembered body parts of her murdered husband, Osiris, and used her magical powers to conceive despite Osiris' death.

Horus was the god of the sky and incorporated both the sun and the moon in his own being: his right eye the sun and his left eye the moon. But that wasn't the full extent of his power. He was known also as the god of war and hunting. Rumour even said that the pharaohs had been incarnations of Horus in human form.

Amos was sitting beside her, glancing at the book over her shoulder.

'And I'll tell you something else,' he said. 'Horus had four sons.'

'You're kidding me!'

'Fact! It's true—isn't it, Larry?'

Larry, whose seat faced them, was enjoying this.

'True,' he said. 'It makes you think Amos must be the real thing after all.'

'But of *course* I'm the real thing,' Amos declared. 'How could you doubt it?'

There was just enough of a twinkle in his eye to show that he was joking.

Halfway through the journey they stopped for lunch. Jackson looked for Freya, meaning to sit beside her at the table, but Larry got there first, immediately engaging her in laughing conversation. To his dismay he noticed that Larry was showing signs of being a fervent admirer, which Freya seemed to enjoy. It worried him because he knew Larry was a man any sensible woman would refuse to take seriously.

When it was time to get back into the coach for the last lap Debra parked herself very firmly next to Jackson, while Larry drew Freya to sit beside himself.

'You're Jackson's sister, aren't you?' he said.

'His stepsister. My mother is married to his father. There's no blood relation between us.'

'I was wondering of you knew the truth about the story that's been whispered about him for the last few years.'

'What story?'

'Something about one of the early TV documentaries he did. It was right at the start of his career and he had an explosive row with the producer. Nobody seems to know the details, but he dug his heels in so hard that he never worked for that firm again.'

'But how come people don't know more about it?'

'Because the firm won't talk about it and Jackson won't talk about it.'

'You mean it's a scandal?'

'I've no idea, but it certainly sounds as though Jackson's grim, unyielding side was in evidence. He mostly keeps it under wraps, but sometimes he can't. It makes you wonder if there was a Horus the Younger as well as Horus the Elder. Ah, who cares? He's a huge success in front of the cameras.'

'And what else matters?'

They shook hands triumphantly. Neither of them noticed Jackson, looking back at them from a few seats away.

Soon they were all keeping watch through the windows for the first sight of Edfu, a smallish city on the left bank of the Nile.

Freya liked it as soon as they arrived. There were cars, as befitted a modern city, but the roads were also filled with carts drawn by horses, giving the place a friendly air.

They were booked into a small hotel next to the river, with rooms overlooking the water. Here too she had a balcony, but Jackson wasn't next door. Her neighbours were Amos and Janine—which, she told herself, she should be glad of.

Drifting out onto the balcony, she found Janine looking down at the street.

'I'm glad you're close to me,' Janine said. 'I really need you.'

'Is Amos being more difficult than usual?'

'You've seen how he is: he's really enjoying this. But there's something else—something I can't define.'

'Is he still giving you funny looks?'

'Yes, but there's more—a new atmosphere that's never been there before. He keeps asking me what I think about things. In the past he hardly ever asked my opinion. It's almost as though he's lost confidence.'

'Him?' Freya echoed sceptically. 'I haven't seen that.'

'No, it only happens when he's with me. Others see only the Amos who's always convinced he's right. But there's another Amos, and for some reason he's not so sure of himself. I get glimpses of him, but then he hides away again.'

'I remember you saying that he's more vulnerable than anyone suspects.'

'Hush, keep your voice down. He must never know I said that.'

'Perhaps it would be good for him to know.'

'Amos couldn't cope with the knowledge that anyone thought him vulnerable. Let's go down and have something to eat.'

Downstairs they found a stall selling books

about Edfu in several languages for tourists. Amos snapped up three and plunged into them at the table.

'It says here,' he declared, 'that the Temple to Horus is the most completely preserved temple remaining in Egypt. They must have realised how much it matters.'

He switched to a page containing a photograph of the temple taken from the air.

'It's huge,' Freya breathed. 'All those sections— the Festival Hall, New Year Chapel, Hall of Offerings, Sanctuary of Horus.'

'And look at those shapes carved into the wall,' Janine said. 'What are they?'

'The one on the left is a king,' Amos explained. 'The one closest to him is Horus, and the one standing behind him is the goddess Hathor— Horus' woman. The small one is their little son, Ihy. The King is making an offering to them, to show his respect.'

'Of course,' Jackson said. 'His power was immense and his influence spread over centuries. Meeting him is going to be really something.'

'Yes,' Amos said. 'Oh, yes.'

Amos said little for the rest of the meal, but the

smile stayed on his face. When Freya suggested an early night to prepare him for the demands of the following day he made no objection.

'Good idea,' Jackson said.

'What about you?' she ventured to ask.

'No chance of an early night for any of us. Too much work still to do.' He laid a hand on her shoulder. 'Get some sleep. Tomorrow will probably tire you.'

She nodded and patted his hand. They had reached their comfort zone again.

Next morning everything was forgotten except the excitement that awaited them. As soon as the coach started Amos produced one of the books he'd bought the night before and went carefully through it, noting all the places to see—especially the Hypostyle Hall, where a statue of Horus was to be found.

'I thought he was a man with a falcon's head,' Freya said, looking over Amos's shoulder at a picture in the book. 'That just looks like a bird.'

'That's how he's represented in statues,' Jackson said. 'Just as a bird—like the model I brought home, except a lot bigger. But in the temple you'll see etchings of him on the walls, and in those he's a man with a falcon's head.'

When they reached the temple they headed for the spot and found what they were looking for.

'Get a load of that!' Larry breathed, staring up at the falcon-shaped statue which loomed over them a good twenty feet.

'I hadn't expected it to be so big,' Freya murmured.

'But of course,' Amos said. 'He has to be majestic.'

They moved on to where there were pictures carved into the wall and found the one they had seen in the book, in which Horus was receiving tribute from royalty. As Jackson had said, here he was a man with a falcon's head. Behind him stood the goddess Hathor, a beautiful woman with a magnificent headdress. Around her neck she wore an elaborate necklace.

'She was known as the cow goddess,' Jackson explained. 'She has a woman's face, but those two curving horns you can see on her head are a version of cow's horns. The orb between them represents the world.'

'She too was great and glorious,' Amos observed. 'She embodied motherhood, feminine love and happiness.'

'And she was his wife?' Freya said.

'That's right,' Amos said, taking Janine's hand in his. 'The most valuable wife and goddess a deity ever had. He gave her that necklace, you know, to show how much he valued her.'

He inclined his head towards Janine. She smiled back, looking a little surprised. Amos's words might almost be described as sentimental—an unusual departure for him.

Jackson too was looking surprised, and he said, 'Actually, it's not that simple. In some legends she was his wife, but in some she was his mother.'

'I thought Isis was his mother,' Freya said.

'It depends whether you're talking about Horus the Elder or Horus the Younger.'

'There really were two?' Freya queried.

'Father and son. That's the fascinating thing about the ancient Egyptians. They could believe and understand several versions of a legend at once.'

'Good for them,' Amos said. 'There's nothing more useful than being able to manipulate the facts—without being too obvious about it, of course.'

'I don't dare ask what you mean by that,' Jackson said, grinning. 'But I'm sure the markets would be interested.'

Amos gave a cackle and slapped his son on the shoulder.

'Horus the Elder and Horus the Younger,' he said. 'What a splendid idea!'

After that he had the time of his life exploring the temple.

'It's really going well,' Jackson said, falling into step with Freya on their way back to the coach. 'Amos doesn't seem at all weak any more.'

'You're right. I think I may be able to return home soon.'

'Don't be in a rush. You should be having a good time out here.'

'No, I'm just getting in the way of your work. You'll be glad when I'm gone.'

'I'll be glad when I'm not being snubbed by you for no reason,' he said wryly. 'I thought we were friends again?'

'We are. I'm not snubbing you. I have an important reason for needing to get home.'

'I see. Should I be happy for you?'

'No,' she said vaguely. 'It's nothing like that.'

'You mean it's not another guy?'

'I mean it's nothing I'm prepared to talk about.'

'But it's important?'

'Yes.'

She hurried away, leaving Jackson staring after her, wishing he could sort his brain out one way or the other. But with Freya that was increasingly difficult.

And he was beginning to fear that it wasn't his brain that caused the problems.

For some reason Freya couldn't quite enter into the spirit of the evening when they all met downstairs for supper. She chatted with Amos, encouraging his triumphant mood at the memory of his encounter with Horus, and she reassured Janine that all was well with her husband. But as the evening drew on she knew that something was missing between them.

Tommy, Larry's irritating second-in-command, was at his liveliest and most tiresome, flirting madly with every female in the group and finally announcing his intention of kissing each of them, one by one.

The others smiled with pleasure at the thought, but Freya shied away.

'I'm leaving,' she said.

'Oh, you're not going now, are you?' Tommy said, confronting her as she rose. 'Just one little kiss.'

'Not me. Please get out of my way.'

'The others were nice about it. Why can't *you* be nice?'

'I'm not nice,' she told him coldly. 'And if you don't stand aside I'll make you regret it.'

But Tommy obviously didn't believe her. He lunged. She ducked, but not in time to avoid him. His lips brushed over hers, lightly, but enough to horrify her and to make Jackson furious.

'That's enough,' he said, seizing Tommy in a fierce grip. 'Get out before I make you sorry.'

'Ah, c'mon, it's just a joke. Freya understands— don't you, Freya? Freya? Where's she gone?'

Where Freya had stood a moment earlier there was only a space.

'She ran out through that door,' Larry said.

'I'll get you for this,' Jackson snapped at Tommy.

'OK, OK…no need to get violent.'

'There's every need. But I'll deal with you later.'

He ran out of the door, looking right and left. There was no sign of Freya, but the door to the street was half open. Frantically he dashed through it, and saw her on the far side of the road.

'Freya!' he yelled. She stopped and looked back at him. 'Come back here, *now.*'

He couldn't tell if she'd heard him above the noise of the street, but she turned away and plunged down a side street, vanishing at once. Jackson darted across the road, causing cars to stop abruptly and horns to blare. He didn't hear them. All his attention was taken up by the chase and his fear of losing her. He ran down the road she'd taken and just saw her at the other end before she vanished behind a building.

An alarming sense of *déjà vu* overtook him. Once before he'd chased someone down side streets, losing him in the distance. The result had been a catastrophe. Driven by desperation, he raced to the far end, just in time to catch a glimpse of her before she vanished again. He tore on and this time luck was with him, for she'd run into a dead end and he caught her as she turned back.

'You crazy woman!' he cried, seizing hold of her. 'Of all the daft things to do! Suppose you'd got lost in these streets? How would you have found your way back? Stupid! *Stupid!*'

'I'll come back when I'm ready,' she said. 'Just let me go!'

'Not in a million years,' he snapped, tightening his grip.

'I said, let me go.'

'And I said no. Do you want to make a fight of it here in the street?'

'If I have to.'

A noise from behind Jackson made them both freeze and turn to see a policeman. He'd plainly heard them speaking, for he addressed them in careful English.

'You don't treat a woman like that,' he said. 'I arrest you.'

Freya drew a sharp breath. 'No,' she said. 'There is no need.'

'This man attacked you.'

'No—it's a misunderstanding.'

'You do not mind that he attacked you?'

'It's not like that.'

He studied them, undecided. Jackson placed both hands on Freya's shoulders.

'We are a couple,' he said. 'We belong together.'

The policeman spoke to Freya. 'You do not wish to be rescued from this man?'

'No, he isn't dangerous,' she said. 'But I thank you for your concern.'

He nodded and backed away. They watched until he was out of sight. Then Jackson blew out his lips in relief.

'Thank you,' he said. 'That could have ended badly.'

'Oh, heavens! I'm so sorry.'

'No need for you to be sorry. Let's just get away from here.'

He hailed a horse carriage that was passing by. It stopped and he helped her aboard, calling to the driver, 'Just take us to the river.'

He got in beside her and they moved off.

'Are you all right?' he said after a while.

'Yes, it's just—oh, goodness! If only—'

'Don't try to talk just now. Let's just ride quietly.' He touched her arm. 'You're shaking,' he said.

'I know. Everything happening suddenly like that—it took me by surprise. I guess I didn't cope very well.'

'Come here.' He put both arms around her, drawing her close so that she rested her head on his shoulder.

At last there was peace, she thought, feeling the strength and comfort he had to offer.

'I'm sorry,' she said again. 'I never meant to get you into trouble.'

'Don't worry. You rescued me in time.'

'You rescued me, you mean. Do we have to go back just yet? I can't face the way they'll all look at me. I'll bet they're laughing fit to bust.'

'Let them laugh. What do we care? We'll stay out awhile and give them time go to bed first.'

They had reached the river now, and sat quietly watching the water glide past.

'I blame myself,' he said. 'I shouldn't have let Tommy get near you. Especially when—well, when you have other interests in your life now.'

He was referring to the hint she'd dropped earlier about having an important reason to get home. She'd refused to say more but he had no doubt of her meaning. Another man had come into her life. She wasn't ready to confide in him, but perhaps he could hope to urge her a little.

When she didn't reply he sighed and continued, 'If Tommy gives you any more trouble just tell me and I'll deal with him. Promise.'

'I don't think he'll trouble me again. You really scared him.'

Yes, he thought. He'd scared Tommy because he'd meant to. He'd been driven by rage at the sight of Freya's distress. Nor had the sight of her being handled by another man improved his temper.

For a while they gazed at the river, until Jackson said, 'Let's have a stroll.'

Leaving the carriage, they walked along the bank until they came to a little café with tables in the open.

'Let's have a coffee,' he said. 'To tell the truth, you're not the only one who needs time before we go back. Tonight something really weird happened.'

She waited until they were seated comfortably before saying, 'What happened?'

'When I was chasing after you through those confusing streets it was as though time had slipped back.' He stopped, embarrassed. 'No, you don't want to hear about that.'

'Yes, I do. Where did time slip back to?'

'Your wedding day. When Dan jumped out of the car and ran. I went after him but he vanished into side turnings until I couldn't see him any more. And then tonight—'

'I did the same,' she said with a little smile to show there were no hard feelings.

'It was eerie—like being part of a ghost story.'

She patted his hand. 'It's not like you to be afraid of ghosts.'

'I wasn't before. I think I am now. You can be like a ghost yourself.'

'You don't mean you're afraid of me?'

'Not exactly. But sometimes I think I could be. It depends on you.'

The arrival of a waiter made them fall silent. While he poured the drinks Freya mused over his words, wondering if she had the courage to pursue them further. Sadly, she realised that she didn't. Not yet, anyway.

When the waiter had departed she said lightly,

'Not all ghosts are evil. Sometimes they're friendly—like the one who's just appeared in my life.'

There it was again he thought, the glancing reference to another man. And suddenly he couldn't bear to be shut out of her confidence a moment longer.

'Is it anyone I know?' he asked.

'Oh, yes, it's someone you know, and when I tell you the name you won't believe me.'

Out of sight, he drove his nails into his palm.

'Tell me,' he said. *'Tell me who it is.'*

CHAPTER EIGHT

'ALL RIGHT, ALL RIGHT,' Freya said in a soothing voice. 'No need to get agitated.'

She didn't know it but there was every need. Agitation was growing in him with alarming speed. He hated her having another man, but most of all he hated his own reaction.

'Just tell me who it is,' he said.

'And stop giving me orders.'

'I'm not giving you orders. I'm pleading with you. Don't you recognise the difference?'

'*Is* there a difference? When a man says *please* isn't it mostly an act, to hide the fact that he's not giving you a choice?'

'Is that experience talking?'

'Yes, it is. Dan used to do it—and Amos too. I hear him talking to my mother. When he says, "Please, my dear…" there's always a slightly ironic note that means he's really saying, *stop wasting time arguing.*'

'And of course you've decided that I'm tarred with the same brush as my father?'

'Well—'

'Come on, we've discussed this before, so let's have the truth. In your eyes I'm as big a bully as he is—just a bit more cunning in how I go about it.'

'Look, I'm sorry, I—'

'Too late to be sorry. My Amos side has taken over. Tell me what I want to know or I'll do something violent.'

'Oh, yeah? Such as what?'

'Such as this,' he said, and stamped his foot hard on the ground. *'Ouch!'*

'Is that the best you can manage?'

'I'm afraid so,' he said, pulling off his shoe and rubbing his foot.

'Have you hurt yourself?'

'Yes—my ankle and further up. Ouch! *Ouch!*'

'I'm not surprised. You slammed it down so hard that the shock must have gone right up your leg. Here, let the nurse do her job.'

She took over, removing his sock and rubbing the foot while he breathed hard.

'That's better,' he said with relief. 'But could you go a bit harder on my ankle? Yes, like that. *Ahh!*'

When she'd done his ankle she moved further up his leg, massaging the calf muscle until its tension relaxed.

'Thanks,' he said at last. 'I think I'll survive now.' He pulled on his sock and shoe, saying wryly, 'Perhaps I'd better give violence a miss in future.'

'Yes, you're not very good at it, are you? I guess it just doesn't come naturally to you.'

'Oh, I don't know. In the years we've known each other I can remember a dozen times when I've wanted to thump you.'

'But you never did. Admirable self-control.'

'Self-control, nothing. I was just scared of how hard you'd thump me back.'

'You do me an injustice. I'm a nurse.'

'But a nurse would know exactly where to thump to reduce me to a shivering wreck.'

'Don't tempt me.'

'Yes, ma'am. No, ma'am. Whatever you say, ma'am,' he said, saluting vigorously. 'Why are you laughing?'

'I was thinking suppose that policeman came upon us again just now.'

'The one who thought I was attacking you?'

'Yes. Imagine how confused he'd be.'

He joined in her laughter before saying, 'I'd have to explain to him that Freya the goddess has all sorts of secret knowledge and skills that she keeps to herself, and that the rest of us had better be very careful. Including him.'

Freya regarded him fondly, relieved and happy that their old, jokey relationship was coming back.

'So, do you still want me to tell you the name of the ghost whose appearance has transformed my life?' she asked.

'I'd kind of like to know.'

'You'll never believe it.'

A sudden dread struck him. 'Oh, no! Tell me it isn't Dan. Freya, you couldn't—'

'No, of course I couldn't. It's not Dan. It's Cassie.'

He stared, astonished into silence. 'What— what did you say?'

'I said Cassie.' Freya regarded him with her

head on one side, enjoying his look of stunned bafflement.

'Cassie? You mean Marcel's wife? I don't understand. How can—?'

'Before I left London Cassie called to tell me something that will make a world of difference to me. Did you know that Amos was so set on me marrying one of you that he actually gave me a large sum of money?'

'I heard a rumour, but I wasn't sure. I suppose he was hoping that one of us would marry you to get our hands on it. How did he think that would make you feel?'

'Does he worry about how people feel as long as they do what he wants?' she asked ironically. 'The odd thing is that he's not an unkind man. He does care about people's feelings—in his own way. But his way is to assume that they'll only be happy if they do what he plans for them.'

'Yes, I know. He's always been like that. So now you'll be a prosperous woman in your own right. You should go out and live the high life on the money. That would teach him.'

'Yes, I could do that now—because I'm beginning to get it back.'

'Get it back? What happened to it?'

'Marcel was having money problems at the time, and Amos thought it might make him turn to me. Instead I loaned it to Cassie, so that she could buy into Marcel's property in Paris and then confront him on equal terms. It helped clear the air between them and they ended up married. Amos was livid.'

Jackson gave a crack of laughter. 'He gave you that money so that you would marry Marcel and you actually used it to help Marcel marry Cassie? I've heard of courage, but that beats all. Dad must be pretty annoyed with you, and yet he still wants you in the family.'

'I think he puts it down to a woman's foolishness. He reckons that if I'm his daughter-in-law he can instruct me in better ways.' She chuckled. 'Or perhaps he thinks if he can make me your wife that'll be a way of punishing me. He's probably thinking, *Then she'll find out what a monster Jackson really is. That'll teach her.*'

'Then he's miscalculated,' Jackson said cheerfully. 'You already know what a monster I am.'

'I'll bet there's a lot still to find out.'

'I'll leave you guessing about that.'

'Anyway, are you saying you didn't know about me lending the money to Cassie? Amos never told anyone?'

'Tell people that you made a fool of him? Can you imagine him doing that?'

'No, you're right. But there's more. It was a good investment. The hotel's doing well and Cassie has now started repaying me with interest.'

He stared. 'So she's the ghost?' he whispered, scarcely able to speak.

'Yes, I hadn't expected to get anything back so soon, but some of the money has gone into my bank already and there's more on the way. I'm going to be a rich woman.'

He pulled himself together.

'Aha! So now you're letting me know that if I need a rich wife you're available?'

'Letting you know that I don't need a husband, and that one word out of place will make me take terrible revenge.'

He grinned. 'Nice to get that clear. Except that I already knew.'

'Well, we've always agreed that we drive each other mad.'

'And as long as it's mutual what does it matter? Have another drink.'

He spoke lightly to hide the storm inside. So she *hadn't* found another man. Just a simple misunderstanding, but it had disturbed him to an extent he didn't want to think about. The implications were too troublesome.

He drained his glass, trying to summon up the courage to say what was on his mind. At last he managed it. 'As you said, not all ghosts are evil. But some of them are. One that still haunts me, and always will, is knowing that I did you harm.'

'Jackson, stop it. We talked about this the other morning in the hotel garden. I told you that there was nothing to forgive and we agreed to put it behind us as though it had never happened.'

'But it did happen. Nothing can make it *un*happen. The effect will be with you all your life. And now I'm going to say something that will make you hate me again. I'm *glad* you didn't marry Dan. I'm not glad of the way it happened, but it's best that you didn't marry him. You wouldn't have been happy. There—now you can call me all the names you like.'

As he spoke he gave her a quizzical look.

'I think I may pass that chance up,' she said. 'I know it wasn't your fault that Dan backed off. He was just looking for an excuse and he seized it. That wasn't what I minded most—'

'I know. It was me not telling you everything about how it happened and why he proposed in the first place. But I swear to you, Freya, I was only thinking of you. You were so hurt I couldn't bear to hurt you even more. I never thought of you finding out some other way. You thought I was laughing up my sleeve at you, but I wasn't.'

'I know. I feel I know you better now, and you wouldn't do that. I shouldn't have flown at you, but suddenly everything seemed to get on top of me.'

Her voice faded and against her will she closed her eyes.

'Freya,' he said anxiously. 'You're not coping well, are you? Even all these weeks later you haven't really begun to get over it.'

'Of course I have,' she said with a bright air that didn't fool him. 'I'm managing just fine. It's like it never happened. Dan isn't worth bothering about.'

She was lying, he thought, and not just to him

but, more seriously, to herself. Dan had hurt her more than she could bear, and she denied it as the only way of coping.

He thought of their meeting in the garden, when she had seemed the strong one, offering him comfort. Now he realised that he'd believed too easily. She seemed in control but she was struggling for that strength and the fight was exhausting her.

Bitterly, he blamed himself again. Would she ever be free of that pain? Would he ever be free of his guilt?

'It's not just Dan,' he said. 'It's what I did too. You're still hurting inside but you won't admit it. You think you can hide it from the world. Well, maybe you can with others, but not from me.'

He waited for her to insist that she was all right, as she so often did, but this time her shoulders sagged.

'Tell me,' he said.

'Oh, it's just—' She sighed. 'That idiot Tommy. I wish he hadn't managed to kiss me—even that brief little kiss. Oh, yes, *you* kissed me once, soon after it happened—'

'And I got it wrong again,' he remembered. 'You thought I was taking advantage.'

'I was off my head. You were being kind. I didn't mean what I said.'

'Don't brood about Tommy, Freya. He doesn't count. I don't count. One day you'll meet a guy who knocks you for six. You'll want him, he'll want you, and you'll be so happy you'll forget Dan ever existed.'

'Oh, no! That's not what I'm planning.'

'Does life happen the way we plan?'

'It does if you've got money. I told you—I'm a prosperous woman now. I'm going to become a business tycoon, investing Amos's money where it'll make the most profit. And I won't care about anything else.'

He had a shocking vision of the cold, unfeeling creature she seemed to want to become.

'Stop it, Freya. That's not you talking'

'Really? Then who is it?'

'Someone else that you think you are—that maybe you want to be. But it won't make you happy. You'd need to be heartless, and you're not.'

'You don't know what I'm like. Even I don't know what I'm really like. But I'm going to enjoy finding out. Maybe I'll get Amos to give me some investment advice. He's always wanted me to be his daughter. I'll never be his daughter by marriage, but I can please him another way.'

'By being his daughter of the heart, you mean?' Jackson asked wryly.

'His daughter of the brain. That's the bit that counts. Neither he nor I has much of a heart.'

'Stop it!' he said fiercely. 'Don't talk like that. Don't even *think* like that. Don't you realise it'll never make you happy?'

'And what *will* make me happy? Another man? I don't think so. It's best to go my own way, keep my fate in my own hands. From now on my life is going to be governed by *my* decisions.'

'If that worked out it would make you stronger than the rest of us. Nobody's life is governed solely by their own decisions, Freya. Don't you know that by now?'

'I should do, shouldn't I? But at least I'll have some kind of control.'

'I imagine Dad thought that, when he gave you money so that you'd marry Marcel. But he was fooling himself—as you showed him.'

'Yes, I did, didn't I? My first success as a businesswoman. The world should beware.'

'Perhaps you're the one who should beware,' he said gently. 'Now, I think we should go. You need some rest.'

He drew her to her feet, supporting her, and they strolled slowly back along the river, his arm about her shoulders. He felt passionate relief that the atmosphere between them had eased and she seemed willing for them to be close again. But he saw more trouble on the horizon.

Freya was vulnerable, and all the more so because she seemed unable to understand just how vulnerable she was. But he saw it clearly, and his old protective instinct rose up again. It was about to make him do something that he knew was a risk, but he was going to do it anyway. For her sake.

Soon the hotel was in sight. He stopped and drew her into the shadows.

'Look at me,' he said.

She raised her head so that her face was illuminated by the moon. He thought he'd never seen anything lovelier.

'Freya, I'm your friend. You do believe that, don't you?'

'Yes, I believe it now.'

'Then take this as an act of friendship,' he whispered, brushing his lips against hers.

He felt her tense and drew back an inch.

'This is to make you forget about that kiss from Tommy,' he said. 'Only that. Do you understand?'

'Yes,' she murmured. 'Yes—'

He laid his lips on hers again, lightly, touching her just enough for her to feel him while keeping his inner self far back in the shadows. He didn't seek a response from her, either from her flesh or her emotions. He had no wish to intrude on her heart. He meant only to drive away the memory of the man who'd troubled her tonight.

'All right,' he said softly. 'Time to go in.'

She followed his lead into the hotel, not speaking. At the door to her room she turned a puzzled gaze on him.

'Goodnight,' he said. 'Sleep well.'

She backed into her room, still not speaking, not taking her eyes from him. When the door was closed Jackson turned away, prey to a wild confusion of thoughts and feelings.

But then, to his annoyance, he saw the last thing he wanted to see. Tommy was standing there in the corridor.

'What the hell are *you* doing here?' Jackson snapped.

'Look, I just came to apologise. I didn't mean things to happen like they did. I didn't know that you and she were—you know—a couple—'

'Shut up!' Jackson told him. 'Do you hear me? *Shut up!*'

Tommy didn't reply. One look at the murder in Jackson's eyes was enough to make him flee.

Janine came to Freya's room early next morning as she was getting dressed.

'Amos has already gone downstairs,' she said. 'He wants to look over the tourist shop again. I can tell that he's got something fixed in his mind, but he won't tell me what.'

'He really enjoyed yesterday,' Freya observed.

'Yes, I haven't seen him so cheerful for a long time. He was on the phone last night to England, I think. I didn't hear everything, but what I did hear sounded businesslike.'

'He's not still doing business, surely? Isn't he retired?'

'He still has a lot of investments, and he likes to stick his nose in. I don't know—I've just got a funny feeling.' She looked curiously at her daughter. 'Freya, are you listening?'

'Yes—yes, of course.'

'You look as if your mind was on another planet.'

'Sorry, I just got distracted.'

'Are you all right, darling?'

'I'm fine,' she said quickly. 'It's just that it's going to be a busy day and there's a lot to think of. Shall we go downstairs?'

Once downstairs she might escape her mother's all-seeing eye. To say that she was distracted was putting it mildly. She been devastated ever since she'd left Jackson the night before.

It had all seemed to go so well. They had cracked jokes with each other, just as in the past. The resentment that had once smouldered in her had faded and it had seemed that their friendship was being restored.

Then he'd kissed her and everything had changed.

The touch of his lips had sent tremors through her, making her heart beat with a force that had taken her by surprise. She'd wanted to cry out in protest. Such things no longer had a place in her life. She was resolved on that and no man was to be allowed to change it.

But the pleasure that had surged through her body couldn't be denied. It had prompted her to yearn towards him, returning the kiss, increasing her own desire and seeking to inspire it in him.

Yet he'd uttered those ominous words. *'Act of friendship.'*

She'd agreed—'Yes—yes…'—but the words had been spoken mindlessly.

When he'd released her she'd somehow kept control of herself, walking and talking like an automaton until she was in her room and the door was safely closed between them. But inside she had been shattered by what had happened to her feelings. Jackson had acted as a kind friend. He'd been careful to make that clear. But her own reaction had been everything she didn't want it to be—everything she didn't want to admit.

Had he sensed her response? The thought made

her cringe with humiliation. Whatever it cost her, he must never be allowed to suspect.

It won't last, she told herself. *Just a momentary reaction. It'll pass and things will be all right.* She was still repeating this assurance to herself as she went downstairs with Janine.

The route to the breakfast room lay past the tourist shop. Through the glass door they could see Amos, talking earnestly to an assistant. He saw them, waved, and came out empty-handed.

'You didn't buy anything, then?' Janine said.

He grinned. 'Let's say I'm thinking about it. Shall we go?'

He went ahead to the breakfast room, walking with the lofty air of a man who had a victory to celebrate. Janine and Freya exchanged baffled glances before following him.

Jackson was there ahead of them, indicating for Freya to sit beside him.

'My leg's still hurting a bit,' he murmured. 'You couldn't bear to give it another rub, could you?'

'You don't need me,' she said. 'I'm sure the hotel has a good doctor.'

'Just a little rub?' he pleaded.

Once she would have agreed without question.

Now the thought of touching him like that made her inner self back off. She *must* not touch him. She didn't dare.

'Sorry, Jackson, I won't have time. I've got to stay close to Amos.'

'He seems fine to me.'

'That's when I have to be most careful. I think I'll go and sit beside him.'

He clasped her hand, preventing her from leaving.

'Have I offended you?'

'Of course not. Don't be silly.'

'You're acting like you're cross with me. If it's about—'

'It's not about anything. Stop being melodramatic.' Her sense of humour came to her rescue. 'Or I shall do something violent.'

'I dare you.'

'Don't. You'll regret it. Now, let me go. I have to go to my patient.'

'But I'm your patient too.'

'You'll be a patient with singing in his ears in a minute. Let go.'

'Oh, all right.' He leaned a little closer to whisper, 'Bully.'

'Not a bully. Just a woman who can take very good care of herself and doesn't need anyone else.'

She slipped away to the next table, where Amos was sitting. But she couldn't resist glancing back at Jackson, and was both dismayed and enchanted to find him watching her with a look of confusion.

CHAPTER NINE

FOR THE REST of that day Amos's behaviour was mysterious. When the others were ready to leave he delayed them while he paid another visit to the tourist shop. Once more he emerged smiling mysteriously, refusing to tell anyone what he was up to. Plainly he was enjoying himself.

At the temple he wandered off alone, insisting that now he knew the place well enough to cope. It seemed to be true, for when Freya and Janine went looking for him she found him before the carved wall picture that they had seen on the first day.

There was Horus, the man with a falcon's head. There was his wife, Hathor. There was the King, respectfully offering them gifts. And there was Amos Falcon, regarding them all with a look of blissful self-satisfaction.

Even as they watched he burst into a laugh that was half a giggle, giving a thumbs-up sign to the wall. Something was making him almost dance with glee. Which wasn't necessarily a good sign.

His cell phone rang. He seized it.

'Yes? Yes? It's all right? You've got it? Great. Let me know when— OK…fine, fine!'

He thrust it back into his pocket, then rubbed his hands with delight and satisfaction.

'Let's go,' Freya muttered, drawing Janine away. 'I can't believe he's actually doing business deals out here.'

'It's more than that,' Janine said. 'It's not just business. He's up to something.'

'Yes, you're right. Come on, Mum. I've got other things to think about than Amos and his carry-on.'

'Lucky you!'

On their return to the hotel Amos again vanished into the tourist shop, then hurried upstairs before they could join him. When it was time for the meal he insisted on going down alone, and they next saw him seated at the table.

Janine went over, but Jackson took Freya's hand.

'What's up with him?' he murmured in her ear.

'He's your father,' she murmured back. 'Surely you know him well enough to read his mind?'

'I think Janine understands him better than anyone.' He gave a wry smile. 'That's why she sometimes gives him a hard time. She knows the best way to deal with him is to stand up to him.'

'That's the best way to deal with any man,' she said lightly.

'Ah, yes, kick him in the teeth at regular intervals, whether he deserves it or not.'

'Some men *always* deserve it,' she observed.

'Why doesn't that surprise me?'

'I can't think. I'd better go now. Amos is waving for me to go and sit with him and Mum.'

It was a cheerful meal. The trip was going well, and only a couple of days were left before they would leave.

At last Amos rose to his feet.

'Before we say goodnight I have something to say.'

They all regarded him with curiosity. Amos took a moment to be sure he had everyone's attention, then began to speak.

'Yesterday we all met Hathor, wife of the falcon god. Naturally she made a huge impact on me.' As he'd done before, he inclined his head towards Janine. 'I particularly noticed her splendid jewellery,' Amos continued. 'So appropriate for a woman of her power and magnificence. It must have been a gift from Horus. And, since he and I are undeniably connected, I felt it was only right to follow his example.'

Amos leaned down, drew a large box out from under the table, and opened it to gasps from everyone at dinner. Inside was a large necklace of gold, studded with rubies, emeralds and sapphires. One look was enough to make clear that they were genuine. The falcon god didn't waste time on imitations.

'Stand up, my dear,' Amos commanded Janine.

Dazed, she did so, and stood while he draped the necklace about her neck, then stepped back and made a flourishing gesture towards her.

'For Hathor, queen of heaven and queen of goddesses,' Amos declared. 'In tribute to her beauty and greatness. She lives by Horus' side, and it is only with her help that he can rule the world.'

Everyone applauded, and some of them cheered. Janine blushed and seemed overcome.

Amos leaned towards her and Freya could just make out that he'd murmured, 'Say something.'

She replied softly, 'In front of all these people?'

'Of course. Everyone must know how much you matter to me.'

Blushing, Janine put her arms around him and gave him a kiss. At once the others rose and crowded around her, gazing entranced at the valuable jewels.

'However did you afford those?' Larry asked, dumbfounded.

'No problem!' Amos declared loftily. 'The falcon god can do whatever he chooses.'

More applause.

Then Amos continued, 'And that's not all. There are also these.'

He produced two large earrings and a bracelet, all of them matching the fabulous necklace. There were more gasps as he draped them about his wife and stood back with a flourish.

'Thank you, my dear,' she stammered, apparently overcome. 'They are beautiful—so beautiful.'

'Take them as a tribute to the best wife in the world,' he declared loudly. 'No, not the world—

the universe.' He threw out his arms. 'From Horus to Hathor, until the end of time.'

He stretched out a hand and Janine laid her own hand into it. He led her around the table so that everyone could have a good look, then swept her out of the room.

There were astonished murmurs. Most of the people around the table were very impressed. Only Jackson looked wry and thoughtful. And Freya was still a little unsure of her own feelings. She couldn't be sure of anything until she'd talked to Janine.

She slipped away. Upstairs, she went to the room shared by Amos and Janine and knocked. Amos opened the door.

'Doesn't she look wonderful?' he trumpeted, standing back to let her in.

'Marvellous,' Freya agreed as Janine paraded for her. 'Those jewels are so beautiful.'

'And worthy of Hathor,' Amos proclaimed.

Janine twisted and turned into positions that showed off the glittering stones. She was smiling, but Freya could sense something was not quite right. She offered extravagant admiration, embraced her mother, then Amos, and escaped.

It was no surprise when a knock at her door an hour later announced Janine's arrival.

'I slipped out when he'd fallen asleep,' she said. 'I hope I didn't wake you?'

'It doesn't matter. I had the feeling that you might want to talk. What an evening!'

'Yes, it was lovely. Such a wonderful, generous thing for him to do.'

'But…?' Freya queried. For there was something in Janine's voice that was more doubt than pleasure.

'But—oh, I don't know, darling. I feel guilty for not being happier about it. I'm a really ungrateful cow.'

'That's all right. Hathor is the cow goddess.'

'Yes, *she's* a cow—but I'm not Hathor. I'm Janine. And Amos isn't the falcon god. He's just my husband. If only he saw it that way.'

She spoke with a sigh that made Freya sit beside her on the bed and say, 'You didn't really enjoy it, did you? Most women would have loved being given such a magnificent gift like that in front of everyone.'

'But that's just it. *In front of everyone.* If we'd been alone, just the two of us, and he'd spoken from his heart, it would have meant so much more.'

'Perhaps he thought you'd enjoy being in the spotlight?'

'No, the spotlight was all for himself. He was making a grand gesture and he wanted everyone to know it. What you saw tonight wasn't about Hathor receiving a gift. It was about the falcon god making a splendid gesture in the eyes of the world.'

'But that doesn't mean he doesn't have feelings about it,' Freya protested. 'It's nice that he took the trouble and spent all that money.'

'The money's nothing to him. As for trouble— the shop assistant did all the real work. That's what was going on all day.'

'Mum, why are you so determined to see this in a bad light?'

'Perhaps because I want so badly to believe he did it out of true feelings. But I know Amos too well for that.'

'Maybe there's more to him than you think. Maybe his feelings are true and this is just his way of expressing them.'

'Thank you, darling, but it's not that simple.

Ever since I discovered what he did about Dan I've seen him in a different light.'

'But why? You already knew what he was like.'

'Yes, but that seemed to cast an extra cloud and I can't shake it off. It's terribly confusing. I simply never know what's going to happen next.'

'Mmm…' Freya nodded.

'Goodnight, darling. I won't keep you awake any longer.'

When Janine had gone Freya sat by the window, too restless to sleep. Her mother was right. With Amos you never knew what would happen next. Which was also true of Jackson, she reflected. Recent events had taught her *that* with a vengeance.

The next day work at the temple proceeded well, and suddenly Larry came up with a sizzling idea.

'Horus is a falcon,' he told Jackson. 'You're a Falcon. Your father is a Falcon. The viewers will see the connection between Jackson Falcon and the falcon god, so we'll have to say something. And we'll bring your father on for a quick mention. It won't take over the show, but you can interview him in front of the statue and we'll have a little innocent fun. Do you think he'll be up for it?'

'Oh, yes,' Jackson said fervently. 'I think he'll be up for it.'

As expected, Amos was enthusiastic. The scene was set up quickly, with only a slight hiccup when he tried to insist that Janine should be included.

'If Horus is there Hathor should be there too,' he declared.

Larry would have yielded, but it was Janine who killed the idea.

'You do it, darling,' she told Amos. 'I just wouldn't feel easy in front of the cameras.'

'Oh, nonsense! I'll be there to look after you. You must be part of this.'

'I said no. I don't belong in this. That's it. Finished.'

Janine walked away, leaving him thunderstruck.

'You'd think nobody had ever said no to him before,' Freya murmured from the sidelines, where she was standing with Jackson.

'They've tried, but without success,' he replied. 'Janine can mess with his head so that he doesn't know if he's coming or going. And nobody's ever done that before.'

Things calmed down enough for the project to go forward. The camera was put in place, Jackson conducted a brief, good-natured interview with his father, and everyone was pleased.

But when Freya went looking for Amos afterwards she couldn't find him. Nor was there any sight of him until it was time to leave for the hotel. As soon as he was aboard the coach he appeared to go to sleep—not with his head resting on Janine's shoulder, but turning the other way, leaning against the window.

Freya wondered how much asleep he really was.

She wished she knew what was really going on between her mother and Amos.

Back at the hotel, Amos vanished again. There was no doubt that he was avoiding everyone, but most of all he was avoiding his wife.

Freya found him at last in the garden, drinking coffee alone at a table beneath a tree.

'Can I join you?' she asked, sitting beside him without waiting for an answer.

He nodded and made an unconvincing effort at a smile.

'What's the matter?' Freya asked. 'Tell me what's troubling you, Dad?'

He sighed. 'It troubles me when you call me Dad—after what I did to you.'

'Did to me?' she asked carefully.

'Don't pretend you don't know—about Dan, how I tried to make him back off. If I'd had the sense to keep quiet and— Well, everything would be better.'

She stared, wondering if she could have heard right. Amos, famed for his bullying and self-righteousness, was actually admitting that he'd got something wrong? Impossible.

'You do know what I mean, don't you?' Amos persisted. 'Jackson told you, and you told your mother.'

'How do you know that?'

'I was just outside the door.'

'You were—?'

'I couldn't tell anyone what I'd heard, but I've wanted to tell you I'm sorry. I know how much in love with him you were, and but for me he might have proposed for the right reasons.'

'No, I don't think he would,' she said.

'Then you must really resent me for the way I've made you suffer.'

Out of the corner of her eye she saw Jackson appear and move slowly towards them, remaining in the shadows.

'But I don't resent you,' she said. 'I'm over Dan, and I've even begun to wonder if I was ever really in love with him.'

'That's kind of you, but—'

'No, I mean it. He dazzled me. Suddenly all the lights seemed to come on in my life and everything was different, more exciting. I really enjoyed that, but it's not love. It's a bit like going on an exotic holiday, but it comes to an end and you return to reality. Don't worry about me. My heart's not broken.'

'You don't know how glad it makes me to hear that. And, my dear, before we go back, I'd rather your mother didn't know that I was listening when—well, you know.'

Freya understood perfectly. Janine had spoken frankly about the doubts she sometimes had about him, and he cringed at the thought of admitting that he'd heard that.

'Don't worry,' she said. 'I won't tell her.'

'Promise?'

'Promise.'

'Word of honour?'

'Word of honour,' she repeated, struck by his intensity. 'Ah, here's Mum.'

Janine appeared, laying her hand on Amos's shoulder. 'I wondered where you'd vanished to,' she said. 'Time to go in.'

Before leaving Amos gave Freya a significant look, to remind her of the secret she'd promised to keep. She smiled and nodded. Reassured, he turned away.

When she was alone Jackson appeared from behind the tree where he had been lingering.

'I had a feeling you were there,' she said.

'I'm glad I was,' he said. 'I can hardly believe what I've just heard. He actually admitted that he could have been wrong. Who'd have thought he'd ever admit to hearing that talk you had with your mother?'

'Especially given what she said about him.'

'Why? What did she say? I knew he'd eavesdropped that night, because I saw him. But I don't know what he heard.'

'Mum told me she had some doubts about him…whether they had a future together.'

Jackson whistled.

'You mean she might be thinking of leaving him?'

'That was the hint.'

'But women don't leave Dad. He leaves them. Heaven knows he's left plenty of them over the years.'

'But not any more,' Freya observed. 'Suddenly the positions are reversed and he's the one who might be left. That's why he's seemed so different recently. It must have given him a nasty shock, but only in his pride. I doubt if his feelings were hurt.'

'I don't know. I've often wondered if he feels things more than he lets on, because he sees emotion as a weakness. Of course that's why he swore you to silence. He'd die rather than have Janine know he heard her threatening to dump him.'

'Pride again,' she mused. 'I almost feel sorry for him.'

'And that's something you must never let him suspect.'

'I know. He'd regard pity as an insult. Poor Amos. And yet—Jackson, was I wise to promise not to tell Mum? Will I be able to keep that promise?'

'Well, you know, one of the lessons Dad taught me was that wisdom sometimes lies in knowing when to break your word.'

'Yes, I can imagine him saying that.'

'There may come a day when she's entitled to know. But not just yet. For now there's something I want to say.'

He hesitated, as if unsure how to go on. She gave him a questioning look and he seemed to make up his mind. 'Thank you for being so good to him tonight. The way you told him that everything was all right, that you're not pining for Dan—that was very kind.'

'I'm fond of Amos,' she said. 'Oh, I know I get mad at him sometimes, about his habit of insisting on his own way, but it's nice that he wants me in the family—even if I can't say yes.'

'Was it true? What you told him? That you're over Dan? That maybe you never really loved him?'

'Of course it's true. I've told you before, several times.'

'Yes,' he murmured, almost to himself. 'You keep saying it.'

'I'm not weeping and wailing because a man didn't want me. I've got a life to live, and I'm living it very comfortably on my own. So if Amos ever asks you about me, you tell him that he did no harm and I'm perfectly happy.'

'Fine, I'll tell him he did no harm.'

'And that I'm happy.'

'Are you sure about that?'

'Are you doubting me? I said happy and I meant happy—especially with all that money coming my way.'

'And money equals happiness? You're beginning to sound like him.'

'Well, maybe he gets it right sometimes.'

'Don't!' he said fiercely. 'Don't talk like that. It isn't you.'

'It could be the new me. I told you, I'm exploring new horizons and some of them are great fun. Goodnight, Jackson.'

'Goodnight,' he said as she walked away. 'Goodnight—goodbye? I wonder which…'

They were close to finishing the project. Near the end of the next day Jackson was glad to slip away for a breather.

As if drawn by magnets he wandered to the statue of Horus and stood looking up at it, recalling the first time he'd seen it. A bird elevated in such a way might have looked ridiculous, but it didn't. Rearing up to more than twice his own height, its sharp beak impressive against the sky, it suggested only power and danger.

He thought of Amos, a man with white hair and an elderly face, who carried the same aura. The grasping ferocity that had imbued his life and his career was always there, threatening in the background. In that he was undoubtedly Horus.

The light was fading. The others were almost ready to leave and soon he must join them. But first there was something he must do. Leaning back, so that he could confront the creature rearing above him, he spoke.

'I had to come here,' he said. 'You seem to call me. You're just like my father. He won't leave a fellow alone either. Even after we all grew up he could never understand that we were independent. *"Come here..." "Do that..." "Marry the woman I've chosen for you..."'*

Then marry her, whispered a voice in his head. *You know you're in love with her.*

'No way!'

Yes, you are. You've been trying not to admit it but maybe it's time to face facts. She touched your heart when she clung to you in despair.

'That was because I felt guilty.'

Was that the only reason? Maybe you just like being needed.

'Even if you're right—it's too late now, isn't it? She's still snubbing me. She does it with smiles and charm, but a snub is a snub. I'm being kept firmly on the outside. It's not just because of our quarrel. We've kind of made friends again. But more recently she's backed off since the night I kissed her. I only meant to be kind and free her from Tommy—I did, honestly. I wasn't thinking of anything more.'

Don't kid yourself.

'Well, maybe just a little. All right, more than a little. But she wouldn't look at me after everything that's happened.'

Don't give up so easily. Perhaps your moment has come.

The words were so clear he could almost swear

that a real voice had spoken. Stunned, he turned around, wondering if he was going mad. Overhead Horus maintained his lofty dignity.

'Did you say something?' Jackson demanded of him. 'Let's face it, you're never short of opinions. And you're not the only one.'

This time there was only silence, but something about it made the air throb with warning. Horus was as impressive when he said and did nothing as when he exercised his power.

'All right, I'm going,' Jackson said. 'I don't know if we'll ever meet again, but I do know that you'll always be with me; haunting me, advising me, troubling me. Will I be glad of that or not? I wish I knew.'

He hurried out to the coach. Once inside he sat apart, pretending to be asleep. He wanted no contact with anyone now. The thoughts seething in his head needed to be controlled.

But they wouldn't submit to control. They whirled, endlessly repeating.

Don't give up so easily. Perhaps your moment has come—perhaps your moment has come—your moment has come—

Shut up! he told the ghost. *I make my own decisions.*

But this is *your decision.*

What do you think you know about me?

What do you think you know about yourself?

To his relief the coach was slowing. They had arrived at the hotel.

Once inside, his father pounced on him.

'I've had a marvellous idea,' he said. 'That interview we did went well, didn't it? We could do some more.'

'Dad, we're leaving in a couple of days.'

'But you could persuade them to stay a little longer. We must do it now. Later will be too late. This is no time to be giving up.' He made a theatrical gesture. 'Seize the moment.'

'What—what did you say?' Jackson stammered.

'I said, seize the moment. That's the philosophy I've lived by all my life and it's made me a winner. You should know that by now.'

'But is it that simple?' Jackson asked. 'Surely you must first recognise the moment?'

'Of course. That goes without saying.'

'But can you always tell that the moment has come?'

'A strong man creates the moment.'

'Can you really do that?' he murmured. 'And risk getting it wrong?'

'If a man knows what he's doing, he doesn't get it wrong.'

Jackson considered this for a moment.

'That might work sometimes,' he mused. 'In business. But life isn't all money.' Almost under his breath he added, 'Other things matter.'

'I've told you before, the rules that govern business are the same for the rest of life. It doesn't seem that way but it works out that way. A man has to stand his ground.'

'And risk getting it wrong? Risk losing the moment?'

'Then create another moment. Never admit defeat. Make things happen your way.'

Jackson didn't try to answer this. The conversation had drifted into paths he didn't want to follow. Amos's words were so close to what he had seemed to hear in the temple that it gave him an eerie feeling.

He told himself that it meant nothing. Amos

often talked this way and his own mind had attributed the words to Horus. That must be the answer.

But still he couldn't quite dismiss the feeling of unease.

CHAPTER TEN

IT WAS THE last night. Tomorrow they would start the journey back to Cairo. In the restaurant everyone was celebrating. There were brief speeches of triumph and satisfaction. Somebody proposed a toast to Horus and Hathor, which made them all beam. In reply Amos raised his glass to 'My loyal subjects!' Saying it in a humorous way that made everyone laugh and cheer.

Freya looked at Jackson, sitting on the other side of the table, joining in the toasts, enjoying every moment. He was handsome, she had to admit. More handsome than any other man at the table. And others seemed to think so too, because Debra passed him by, touching his shoulder, claiming a friendly kiss before passing on.

Again Freya felt the tremor she'd known when his lips had fleetingly brushed hers. She'd banished that memory, but it refused to be dismissed, slipping back at odd moments, warning her that nothing was finally settled. Nor did she want to dismiss it. She felt herself smiling and didn't even try not to.

He glanced up, saw her watching him and answered her smile with one of his own. Did he know what she was thinking? she wondered. Was he remembering the same? Was that the meaning behind his smile?

At last it was time to say goodnight. They began to drift out into the hall and up the stairs. But Freya, overcome by a sudden impulse, slipped out of the front door. She wanted to be alone, to walk by the river, to give herself up to memories that she must defy yet could enjoy one last time.

There along the bank was the place where Jackson had kissed her, tenderly brushing his lips against hers as an act of kindness and friendship. How many times had she reminded herself of that? How often had she warned herself not to hope for anything else? How often had she called herself a coward for being determined to avoid love for the rest of her life, or resist it if it couldn't be avoided?

Here was the place. Here, if nowhere else in the

world, she could allow herself to remember the forbidden feelings and revel in them.

'*This is to get rid of Tommy,*' he'd said. '*Only that. Do you understand*?'

He'd tried to protect her from responding to him. And he'd failed.

Closing her eyes, she leaned against the rail, raising her face to the glowing moon, and allowed the tremors to run through her again.

For the last time, she promised herself. The very last time.

At last she opened her eyes.

He was there.

At first she thought he was a delusion, but then she realised that Jackson was standing there, just a few feet away, watching her.

'I guess we both had the same idea,' he said, coming towards her.

'We both—?' Her heart was beating with either hope or disbelief. Or perhaps the two of them.

'Coming out here,' Jackson said. 'I had to take a walk along the river. I've loved this place and I'll be sorry to leave. I'm glad you feel the same. It's a pity you didn't summon me to come with you. If you say you don't want me I'll go away.'

'No, don't do that,' she said quickly. Pulling herself together, she assumed a nonchalant demeanour. 'I just thought you were tired and wanted to get to bed.'

'Meaning I'm a wimp? Thank you, ma'am. No, I wouldn't want to miss a last look here. It's a lovely place.'

Freya had command of herself now and managed to say lightly, 'It's affected us all in so many ways. Amos, my mother…. Things seem so different between them now.'

'Yes, ever since he learned that she had her doubts about him. Perhaps it explains that dramatic gift to "Hathor". She's got him worried. He won't admit it, but he's trying to bind her to him.'

'But Mum didn't marry him for his money and she isn't a woman to be impressed by grand gestures. If he's trying to win her heart again he's going the wrong way about it.'

'Yes, and he thinks he's being so clever,' Jackson mused. 'That's the trouble. It's easy to think you're being clever when you're actually making a woman despise you.'

She regarded him with her head on one side and a teasing smile on her face.

'Despise you? I shouldn't think you have much to worry about in that direction. Your fan base doubles every day, so I hear. I expect Travis is getting quite jealous.'

'Ha-ha!' he said ironically. 'Yes, I have my female fans—women who don't know me, who wouldn't give tuppence for me if they did know me. I'm talking about real relationships. I've never been brilliant at those.' He hesitated before saying, 'There was this girl—it took me too long to realise what we might be to each other, and by the time I did—well, I'd messed up.'

She too paused before speaking, wondering if she'd divined his true meaning.

'So what happened? Has she married someone else?'

'No, but I expect she will.'

'Maybe not,' she said carefully. 'She might have gone off the whole idea.'

'Blaming all men because of one useless dope? That's a bit hard, isn't it?'

'Perhaps she thinks *all* men are useless dopes,' Freya said, elaborately casual.

'She might be right. But some are less dopey than others.'

'And some are more dopey than others.' She laughed softly. 'And some are so hopelessly dopey that it's a waste of time trying to improve them.'

He considered this. 'She shouldn't judge too soon. It might be time well spent.'

'Maybe—maybe not. We might never know.'

'Oh, yes,' he said softly. 'We'll know. Perhaps we already know. But things get in the way. If we let them.'

'If we let them it's because there's no choice,' she said gently.

'Then we'll have to wait and find out.'

She nodded, meeting his eyes directly. It felt good to be here, talking in a mysterious way that might mean something or might not. That would be decided in another world.

Neither of them realised that they were being watched from a window on the second floor of the hotel. Absorbed in each other, they didn't glance up, but began to walk along the river, hand in hand, until they were out of sight.

'Oh, that's lovely,' Janine said, drawing back from the window. 'They look so right together.'

'Of course they're right together,' Amos said.

'I've always said so, but nobody would listen to me.' He gave a deep, self-satisfied sigh. 'I knew it would work.'

'Knew what would work?'

'Getting Freya out here.'

'She came out to look after you because you were unwell.'

'That's what I wanted everyone to think, but there was nothing really wrong with me. I was sure that once she was here they'd get together at last.'

'Nothing wrong with you?' Janine repeated slowly. 'All those breathless attacks—'

'They weren't difficult to stage. I did it to make you both come out here. I knew they'd have to spend a lot of time together.' He gave a rich chuckle. 'And it worked. Oh, come on, don't look at me like that. You know I occasionally bend the facts a little.'

'A *little*?' she breathed. 'This wasn't a little. It was a massive deceit.'

'But it was for a good cause. Wouldn't you like to see them married?'

'Yes—if it's what they both want. But not just because they were manipulated.'

'All I did was give them the chance to be together. Was that wrong?'

'No,' Janine said. 'But you could have confided in me. If you'd told me that your illness was only a pretence—let me be part of it—if only you'd trusted me enough to do that. But you shut me out. Do you know how I've felt since I thought you were ill again? I've lain awake at night, worrying about you. It never once crossed my mind that the whole thing was an act to get your own way.'

She seemed to pull herself up short, and a new, harder note came into her voice.

'But perhaps it should have done. As you say, I know what you're like. I know you don't have a conscience about how you make everyone jump to do your bidding. I even know about how you tried to order Dan to stay away from Freya.'

Amos raised his head to gaze at her with a mixture of astonishment and dismay. For once in his life words did not come easily.

'Yes,' he mumbled. 'Well—'

Janine regarded him curiously. 'Is that all you've got to say? Did you hear what I just told you? I know about what you did with Dan—how you tried to break him up with Freya.'

'Let's leave that,' he said hastily.

'You don't seem surprised. Don't you wonder how I knew?'

'I know Freya told you,' he growled.

'How?'

'I—I happened to be passing the door when she was talking.'

'I see. You "happened" to be passing the door, and then you "happened" to stay there and spy on us. And you heard—?'

'Yes,' he snapped. 'I heard everything.'

Everything. The word seemed to echo in the air. 'Everything' meant he'd heard her remarks about him.

'He likes to see himself as powerful. The trouble is, that's the side of him I find hardest to live with.'

He knew she'd said that. And he'd heard Freya ask why she stayed with him, heard her reply.

'He needs me. He's vulnerable in ways he doesn't realise.'

How he would resent her for daring to suggest that he was vulnerable!

'I heard everything,' Amos repeated now in a harsh voice. 'So I've known all this time that you know about me and Dan. But you never said anything to me about it.'

'What could I say?' she flung at him. 'For a while I tried not to believe it. I didn't want to think that even you would go that far. But in my heart I knew it was true, and I know it even more now that you've told me about the trick you pulled to get Freya out here.'

'I was trying to save her from pain, and I was right. Dan behaved as badly as I knew he would.'

'*You* were the cause of her pain. Dan would never have proposed in the first place if you hadn't made him angry. Don't try to play the saint, Amos. You thought of what you wanted and nothing else, and that's why Freya got hurt. And now she'll get hurt again, because you have to twist everything.'

'Why should she be hurt again? Jackson's a good man. He'll make her a fine husband.'

'Who says she'll marry him? Who says she'll marry any man? Don't you understand that now she sees your sex in a completely new light and it isn't a favourable one? And I can understand that. But you just can't see anyone else's point of view. This latest deception—'

'My dear—'

'Don't call me that. I'm not your dear. I wonder if I ever was.'

'I was only going to say that "deception" is pitching it too strong. I played a little trick, that's all.'

'One trick too many. You really are as unpleasant as people say.'

'Don't make a drama out of this. Perhaps I should have told you that I was pretending, but what would you have done? Helped me? I don't think so.'

'So anyone who dares to disagree with you is banished out into the cold?' She gave a great sigh. 'And that includes me.'

Amos waved his hands helplessly. 'I didn't mean it like that. Look, I'm sorry. But we can put it behind us.'

'Perhaps you can. I'm not sure that I can.'

'But I've tried to show you how much you mean to me. Look at those lovely jewels I gave you.'

'Oh, Amos, you're as blind to the truth about yourself as you're blind to other people. That wasn't a gift to me. That was a parade in the spotlight for you.'

'You were in the spotlight too. Everyone said how marvellous you looked.'

'I didn't want the spotlight. It would have been nicer to be alone with you. But when we got back to our room you couldn't wait to take the jewels off me and lock them away safely.'

He gave a grumpy sigh. 'I don't know what to say to you.'

'You never did,' she told him softly. 'Let's not talk about it any more now. I need to do some thinking about the future.'

'What are you saying?' he demanded. 'We're married. That's the future.'

'Perhaps. Let me think about it first.'

'You'd do better getting some sleep. You're tired. That's what this is all about. Tomorrow none of it will matter.'

But he didn't risk looking at her as he said it. She might have seen the fear in his eyes.

'Perhaps it's time we went back,' Jackson said.

He hailed a horse-drawn carriage and helped

her aboard. For a few minutes they sat enjoying the clip-clopping rhythm. He took her hand in his.

'Freya,' he said softly, 'there's something— I don't know when I'll get the chance to— Please understand and don't hate me again.'

'Hate you for what?'

'This,' he said, taking her into his arms.

At once she knew that she'd wanted this ever since that night. One part of her mind told her she should be cautious and resist him, but everything else in her knew that she would never have forgiven him if he hadn't placed his lips on hers, tenderly but insistently.

Her response was beyond her own control, making her slip her hands up around his neck, then his head, drawing him closer so that her mouth could explore his more thoroughly. He made a soft, sighing sound and increased his fervour.

'Freya?' he whispered.

'Yes— Yes—'

Somewhere at the back of her mind a warning voice tried to say no, but she ignored it. She would be sensible another time, but for now she could only allow her feelings to take over, driving her towards him, ever closer, ever more desirous.

'I've wanted this ever since last time,' he murmured.

'But you said—friendship—'

'I know. But I was wrong. I can't help it. It's there between us and I can't make it go away. *Freya*—'

Whatever answer she might have made was silenced in the renewed pressure of his lips, moving fiercely over hers. Helplessly she abandoned all efforts at self-control and gave herself up to the pleasure that was coursing through her.

It was a kiss of discovery for both of them.

Jackson had followed her out in the hope of making this very thing happen, yet even he was caught off-guard by sensations and emotions. He'd imagined himself prepared for those feelings, but nothing could have prepared him for what was happening deep in his heart and his body.

Horus had warned him that he was falling in love, but even Horus didn't understand everything. The road that stretched ahead was one that he must negotiate by himself. Perhaps with her help.

Freya felt as though everything was whirling about her. What was happening now was exactly what she had vowed she would never allow. But she seemed to have been transported to another world, one where her determination counted for nothing.

She had enjoyed Dan's kisses, but she knew now that he'd never given her this sense of conveying a secret message from his inner self. Willing or not, she responded, moving her lips in soft caresses, sending her own message from a part of herself she'd never known before.

It was like becoming a different person with different thoughts and feelings in a different world. And she knew that she must become this new person—or refuse to become her to her own eternal regret. She must make the decision any moment now, but first she would allow herself to relish the joy that possessed her for one more moment—one more—one more…

'We've arrived,' Jackson murmured. 'Let's slip in quietly.'

They managed to cross the lobby and go up in

the elevator without being seen by anyone who knew them.

At the door of her room she stood, hesitant.

'Can I come in?' Jackson whispered, moving closer.

Unable to speak, she nodded and opened the door. He followed her in, closed the door and immediately took her in his arms.

'I've wanted this,' he murmured. 'I was sure our time must come—and now it has. Don't you feel that?'

She couldn't answer, for he was kissing her again, holding her tighter than before, his eyes, his mouth, his whole body full of intent. The moment was drawing near.

Suddenly she drew a long, trembling breath.

'No. Jackson. Wait.'

'What is it?'

'I—I don't know, but I can't— I'm not ready.'

'We're both ready. This has been waiting for us.'

'No, please—'

'Freya—'

'Let me go.'

'But I—'

'Let me go, *please.*'

She felt a fierce tremor go through him and for a moment she thought he would refuse. But then he dropped his hands and stepped back. He was breathing heavily, and she had the feeling that he was fighting for control.

'I'm sorry,' she said. 'I didn't mean this to happen. But I'm not sure— I need more time.'

'All right,' he said in a rasping voice. 'Don't worry. I'm going.'

'Jackson, I'm really sorry.'

'Don't be sorry,' he said. 'There's still a lot we don't know about ourselves and each other. We'll have time to find out and then—then will be the time for you to make your decision. I'll be waiting for you, and I know you'll come to me. Goodnight.'

She was left looking at the closed door, shaking with the ferocity of her own reaction and the struggle within herself.

She had wanted what was happening. Her whole self had seemed to cry *yes.* But without warning everything had gone into reverse. *Yes* had become *no.*

And the reason, deny it as she might, was fear.

Jackson had said there was still a lot they didn't know. He was right. And one thing she didn't know was whether she could risk falling in love again after the first disaster.

Coward, she told herself scornfully. *You keep telling yourself that you weren't really in love with Dan. And you weren't. You know that now.*

But she'd believed she was at the time. The devastation had been terrible, and too little time had passed for her to recover her courage.

And courage mattered. Instinct told her that it would need every scrap of daring she could find to love Jackson. And just now she wasn't sure she wanted to take the risk.

He'd known how uncertain things were between them, but only she understood how uncertain they might always be.

'I'll be waiting for you, and I know you'll come to me.'

The memory of those words almost made her cry out in anger and frustration.

How certain he was that her decision would be the one he wanted. Before she even knew it herself.

She wouldn't allow herself to think tonight. She

lay down, seeking the release of sleep, but it was denied. Her mind was in turmoil, and after tossing and turning for half an hour she sat up, realising that there were raised voices coming from Amos and Janine's room next door.

She went out. The voices were sharper, revealing that a row was going on.

She heard Amos snap, 'You're making a mountain out of a molehill.'

Then he came storming out and stomped away down the corridor without seeing Freya. Quickly she knocked on the door, which Janine opened, standing back to usher her in.

'Mum, what's happened? What are you rowing about?'

'The way he's behaved to you.'

'You mean that business with Dan? Don't worry, that's history.'

'It's not just that. You'd think he'd learn his lesson about interfering in other people's lives, but no. Not him. He's still trying to marry you off to Jackson.'

'What? Surely not?'

'That's why he got you out here.'

'But he was poorly…he needed looking after—

Oh, no! Tell me what I'm thinking is wrong. He couldn't— He didn't—'

'I'm afraid he did. There was nothing wrong with him. That heavy breathing was an act. He meant you to come out here, spend a lot of time with Jackson, and—oh, well, you can guess the rest.'

Freya banged her hand against her forehead, snapping out a thoroughly unladylike word.

'I don't know why I'm surprised,' she said. 'You said he couldn't surprise me any more. He actually thought that Jackson and I—after everything that's happened—'

'Well, the two of you do seem to be getting on very well again.'

'Only as friends,' Freya said quickly. 'Nothing more. How did you learn what he'd been up to?'

'Earlier tonight we saw you wandering along the riverbank together and he was so pleased with himself that he told me what he'd done—pretending to be ill to get you out here.'

'And you were so worried...' Freya breathed. 'Didn't he understand what he was doing to you?'

'Does he ever understand anything that doesn't suit him?'

'No, never. Well, that's it. He doesn't need me, so I'm going back to England. I don't think I can endure the sight of him any more.'

'I think I'll come with you. I need to put some space between Amos and me while I try to see into the future. Don't go to England. Come to Monte Carlo and stay with me for a while.'

'All right. It'll be good to have some time alone together. Are you seriously thinking of leaving Amos?'

'I don't really know. What I do know is that things between us aren't as I hoped, and I have to mull it over. I need space and to be free of him for a while.'

'Yes,' Freya murmured. 'To be free.'

CHAPTER ELEVEN

As THEY WAITED for the coach the next morning Jackson came to stand beside Freya.

'What's up with them?' he asked, inclining his head to Amos and Janine. Although they were standing together there was an unmistakable air of frostiness.

'They've quarrelled, and this time it's serious,' Freya said. 'She found out that he never was ill. He only pretended to be short of breath.'

'But why?'

'To make me come out here and to get you and me together. He hasn't given up, and this is his latest trick.'

Jackson swore under his breath. 'I could strangle him!'

'Join the queue.'

'How did your mother find out?'

'He told her. Apparently he was so sure the trick had worked that he boasted about it.'

'I should have realised, but I can hardly believe it—even of him. Goodness knows what the atmosphere will be like between him and Janine now.'

'You don't need to worry about that. Mum's going home. She says she needs to get away from him for a while. And I'm going with her.'

'Must you?'

'I can't let her be alone now she's so unhappy.'

'I suppose not, but I wish you weren't going. Ah, well, we'll be finished in Egypt soon. Once we're all back in England things will be better. We can meet and talk.'

'I shan't be in England for a while. I'm going to Monte Carlo with her.'

'How long for?'

'I'm not sure. Certainly until Amos comes home, and maybe a while after that if I think she needs me.'

'But, Freya—'

'Oh, look, Amos is waving at you. Perhaps you should go and talk to him.'

He seemed about to protest, but then he nodded and went over to his father.

Freya joined Janine.

'You were both very quiet at breakfast.'

'I've told him I'm returning to Monte Carlo and he's furious with me. But I'm going anyway. My days of jumping to do his bidding are over.'

'It's news to me that you ever did jump to do his bidding.'

'I tried to please him as often as possible. If I had to refuse him I did it gently, lovingly. But now I have to make a stand. I'm doing what suits me, and if he doesn't like it he can take a running jump.'

'Good for you. I'll call the airport as soon as we reach Cairo.'

On the coach journey they sat together, while Jackson claimed the seat beside his father. Their words were inaudible, but Freya sensed that Jackson was trying to soothe him. She doubted that he was totally successful, but Amos's scowl faded, to be replaced by a look that might have been sadness.

When they reached the hotel in Cairo Freya went straight to the reception desk and asked for a call to be put through to the airport. What followed took only a few minutes.

'There's a plane leaving for Nice tonight,' she told Janine. 'I've booked us on it.'

She heard Amos's harsh gasp and guessed that he'd counted on having this evening to pressurise Janine into staying. But Freya knew her mother's mind was made up. Suddenly everything had changed, making her stronger. Clearly Amos had also sensed that change, but he seemed unable to cope with it. Freya actually found herself feeling sorry for him.

Jackson and Amos came with them to the airport and saw them as far as Check In. Jackson drew Freya aside.

'I wish you weren't going,' he said, his hands gentle but firm on her arms.

'You'll be better without me,' she said. 'I'm a distraction. It's your first job with this firm. You have to give it everything.'

'There's only one thing in the world that can make me want to give everything. All myself. All my heart and soul.'

'Don't.' She laid her fingertips over his mouth. 'Not yet.'

'Not yet? But perhaps some day soon?'

'I don't know,' she said desperately.

'But one thing you do know. I'm yours if you want me. Do you need to know more?'

'I need time. Sometimes things seem so clear and sometimes everything's a wild confusion. Please, Jackson.'

'All right. I guess I can be patient as long as I have some hope. But don't torture me too long. Please.'

'Jackson, I don't— I can't—'

Their boarding call came from the loudspeaker.

'I must go,' she said quickly. 'Goodbye.'

'Goodbye—until we meet again.'

Together the two women walked away through Check In and on to the Departure Lounge. At the end of the corridor they turned and saw the two men still standing there, watching them from a distance.

Freya had an eerie feeling of history repeating itself in mirror image. It was only a few weeks ago that she and Janine had stood together in an airport, watching Amos and Jackson depart. There had been desolation in her heart then, although nothing like what she felt now. It was all so different, and she no longer knew what to think about anything in the world. Including Jackson. Including her own heart.

His words should have made her spirits soar.

Yet to hear his declaration of love when she was walking away from him, perhaps for ever, had sunk her in despair.

I'm mad, she thought. *Mad, crazy, stupid. And I have no idea what to do about it.*

'Are they still there?' Janine asked, straining to see.

'Yes,' Freya whispered. 'Still there.'

'Oh, yes. Look how alike they are. It almost makes you believe in Horus the Elder and Horus the Younger.'

'Don't,' Freya said with a shudder.

'You're right. Let's put them behind us.'

When they had turned the corner out of sight the two men watching them stood for a moment without moving.

At last Amos spoke. 'So that's that.'

'I wonder,' Jackson mused, 'just how often that really *is* that.'

'I know this has got you down, but don't give in to those feelings. Just because a woman goes away it doesn't mean she's abandoned you. Of course she'd like you to think so. It's a power game. You're supposed to go after her. And if you don't, she'll come back to you.'

Slowly Jackson turned his gaze on his father. 'That's what you really think, is it?'

'Just remember, don't be the one to give in. You've got to be strong. That's the rule of life and the rule of love.'

'Unless it backfires,' Jackson murmured. 'And what do you do then? Especially if *she's* playing by different rules, and you don't know what they are.'

Amos gave a snort of derisive laughter. 'Women always play by different rules, and no man ever knows what they are. All you can be sure of is that they'll trip you up if they can.'

'Then I reckon we've both been tripped up,' Jackson observed. 'It's time we were going.'

For much of the flight from Cairo to Nice Freya gazed out of the window at the clouds. By the time they got into the taxi from Nice to Monte Carlo she was ready to sleep. It was a relief to let her mind do nothing.

As the days passed she was glad she'd chosen to be with her mother. It was a long time since they had been alone together, able to talk freely and confide their troubles. It meant facing searching questions from Janine, but they forced her to confront herself and her own confusion.

'You really came with me to get away from Jackson, didn't you?' Janine asked once.

'Yes, I think I did.'

'I thought you two had made up. Have you quarrelled again?'

'No.' She sighed. 'It's not a quarrel. It's sadder than that.'

'If it's not a quarrel, what can it possibly be?'

'I don't know.'

'But it worries you. Darling, if you're falling in love with him don't fight it just to teach Amos a lesson.'

'I'm not falling in love with him.'

'Are you sure?'

'Quite sure,' she said firmly.

'It's just that when it all happened I had the strangest feeling that quarrelling with Jackson hurt you more than losing Dan.'

'Mum, will you let it go, please? I'm not falling in love with Jackson.'

If Janine thought her daughter was trying to convince herself she was too tactful to say so.

'All right, darling,' she murmured. 'Whatever you say.'

'I'm not ready to fall in love with anyone yet,' Freya asserted. 'Maybe never.'

Even to Janine she could not explain the storm of confusion that Jackson caused within her. Part of her yearned towards him, longed for his love. But part of her recoiled from the strength of her own feelings—especially for a man she did not completely trust.

He was too much like Amos—too likely to indulge in deception to achieve his ends. But his charm could make her forget the danger, and his kisses had a power that alarmed her. She missed him terribly, but she also felt safer at a distance.

On the day Amos announced that he would soon be home Freya received a call from Cassie in Paris.

'She's making another repayment to me,' she told Janine, 'and she says that since I'm getting so interested in finance I should visit them and learn some more about it. I've said yes. It'll get me out of the way when Amos arrives. I think the two of you need to be alone.'

'Good idea,' Janine agreed. 'Have a wonderful time in Paris.'

Two days later Freya was comfortably ensconced in a room at La Couronne, the luxurious Paris hotel that Cassie and Marcel jointly owned and where they lived. She plunged into the pleasures of this new life, learning about finance and being treated as an honoured guest.

Jackson called her every day. She talked to him cheerfully, but in a way that revealed no feelings.

'I'm having a wonderful time,' she declared. 'Paris is lovely and I'm really enjoying my new life. Just you wait and see. I'm going to be the businesswoman of the year.'

'I'm sure you can be anything you want. So that's it? You've got the future all arranged?'

'Maybe. I've discovered that you don't arrange the future. It just happens and you try to turn it to your advantage.'

'Very shrewd. Right, I've got to go now. Goodbye.'

'Goodbye,' she said, hanging up. 'Goodbye...'

And it might be goodbye finally. Perhaps that was what the future held. If so, she would do her best to turn it to her advantage.

There was no lack of pleasures available to her. Marcel even had a handsome friend, Pierre, who paid her particular attention.

'I must warn you about him,' Marcel said one evening. 'He needs money, and word's got around that you could afford a few investments.'

'That's what I figured,' she replied. 'Don't worry, I'm in no danger.'

The four of them would sometimes dine together downstairs in La Couronne's restaurant, and Pierre would give a performance of devotion that might have convinced her if she'd wanted to be convinced. As it was, she merely laughed, heard his speeches with a pretence of attention and let him kiss her hand.

'Hey, look who's here.' Cassie said suddenly one evening.

Turning, they saw a man standing nearby, watching them with hard eyes. His gaze was fixed on Pierre, holding Freya's hand to his lips, and a fierce glow seemed to come from him.

It was Jackson.

Marcel rose, greeting his brother cheerfully, bringing him over to the table.

'Great to see you. Why didn't you say you were coming?'

'It was a last-minute decision and I can't stay long. Freya, can we go somewhere?'

'But surely you can have something to eat first,' Cassie protested.

'Thank you, but I can't. Freya?'

'Yes,' she said.

There was no way of refusing this man's fierce intent. The moment had come. The moment that in her heart she had always known would come.

He didn't speak as she led him into the elevator and up to her room. When the door was closed she spoke in a voice that sounded tremulous even to her own ears.

'You gave me a shock, appearing out of the blue like that.'

'Are you surprised that I came here? You shouldn't be. You practically forced me.'

'I didn't force you.'

'When we speak on the phone it's like talking to a stranger. Is that what you want to be to me? A stranger?'

'No, of course not. But—'

'Whenever we've spoken I've felt that you've withdrawn a little further.'

'It's just that I'm very busy.'

'Too busy to spend time with the man who loves you? Don't look so surprised. I told you at the airport that I love you—'

'You didn't actually use the word *love*,' she mused.

'I told you I was yours, heart and soul. If that doesn't mean love, what does it mean? And you must have guessed my feelings before that.'

'I know that we both got carried away. So much has happened that we can't really see each other straight any more. Isn't it better to step back and wait a little?'

'No, it isn't better. And wait for what? For you to let me into your life? I could wait for ever for that. And I won't wait. I love you. I think I've loved you for a long time, and I'd probably have realised it sooner but for Dad. The way he kept trying to force us together just had the opposite effect. But we can't let him do that to us. I've held back, waiting for you to see that we belong with each other not because of Dad but in spite of him.'

'How do you know that we belong together?' she cried. 'Just because it's what you want?'

'No, I think it's what you want too. I feel it when I hold you in my arms. I feel it even more when I kiss you and you kiss me back. I think you love me as much as I love you.'

'You have no right to take that for granted.'

'You think I believe only what I want to believe? All right, why don't you prove me wrong?'

Before she could answer he'd taken her in his arms and was kissing her with an intensity that had a hint of desperation. The instinct to resist him flared for the briefest moment and died before the ferocity of her own feelings. Without wanting to she was kissing him back, moving her lips in ways that she knew challenged him, teased him, taunted him.

'I had to come here,' he said. 'I told myself I was going to be patient, but I can't think of anything but you. I want to marry you. I want you more than I've ever wanted anything in my life. I can't believe that it's all for nothing. Freya, don't tell me it's all on my side. You wouldn't kiss me like that if you felt nothing for me. You're mine. You can't be anyone else's.'

But suddenly the fear was there again, making her struggle free.

"That's the sort of thing Dan said,' she cried. 'And it was all a lie. No, leave me alone.'

'But I want to marry you. I *have* to. I won't give up.'

'Do you know how much like your father you sound when you say that? He announces what he wants and everyone has to fall in line.'

'I'm not my father, and I'm not like him. I'm not doing this to please him. I think I've wanted to marry you for a long time.'

'How long? Was that in your mind on my wedding day, when you drove my groom away? Has that been the truth all the time?'

'Don't say that. Don't even think it.'

'Why shouldn't I say it? You've as good as admitted it.'

'No!'

'That's been the truth all the time, hasn't it? You wanted me so you manipulated everything to get me. I trusted you. I relied on you. I felt I could turn to you. But you've never really been the man I thought you were.'

'If that's what you truly think of me,' he said,

'then I've been wasting my time. We've both been deceived in each other.'

He drew a long, rasping breath.

'I'd better go. If I stay any longer I could start to hate you as much as I love you.'

'Yes, go—*go!*'

He stepped back to the door, opened it, and then paused to say quietly, 'I've never loved anyone in my life as much as I love you. When I understood that it was like the sun coming out in the universe. I felt that nothing could ever be the same again. And it won't be. But I didn't realise it would be like this. Goodbye, Freya. I hope that somehow you find the good life that I can't give you.'

The door closed.

Freya reached out her hands towards it, but stopped, drew back, and threw herself on the bed in a passion of sobs.

Again she had a sense of history repeating itself. After Dan's desertion she'd set herself to build a new life. Now she was rebuilding again, but she knew that Jackson had not deserted her. It was she who had deserted him.

The thought of his pain broke her heart, but she knew she'd had no choice. Something wasn't right between them, and until she understood it and dealt with it there was no way of going forward.

In her darkest moments she feared that there never would be a way.

She tried to distract herself by concentrating on business, learning something new from Marcel and Cassie every day. They both acclaimed her as a splendid pupil.

'I think life as a businesswoman might well suit you,' Marcel observed one evening. 'You've got the shrewdness and clear sight, plus a good head for figures. And you're not easily taken in.'

'You mean I saw through Pierre and the other men who thought they could seduce me and part me from my money?'

'Yes, it was wonderful watching you,' Cassie chuckled.

'They were easy to see through,' Freya said with a shrug. 'Mind you, most men are.'

'Stick with that belief,' Marcel told her. 'You'll end up as a millionaire.'

They all laughed.

He was about to refill their glasses when the phone rang.

'Who can that be at this time of night? Hello? Leonid! Good to hear from you. What's that? Congratulations! How is Perdita? Fantastic!'

'Has she had the baby?' Cassie asked eagerly.

'Yes. It's a girl. Mother and daughter are doing fine.'

'Wonderful!' Freya and Cassie exclaimed, throwing their arms around each other.

After a few more minutes Marcel hung up.

'We're all invited to the christening,' he said.

'Lovely!' Cassie cried. 'I've always wanted to see Moscow. Oh, Freya, won't that be exciting?'

'Thrilling,' she agreed.

It would be good to see Jackson. Things might never again be right between them, but she needed to see his face, watch his eyes, discover the future.

The next day she returned to Monte Carlo, to discover Janine in an edgy mood.

'I hoped things would be better between you and Amos by now,' she ventured.

'He plays the devoted husband, but I'm not

fooled. You only have to look at how eager he is to go to Moscow.'

'But of course. He's going to be a grandfather,' Freya argued. 'The world's going to have another Falcon.' She struck a theatrical attitude. 'An addition to a great dynasty. He must be basking in it.'

'Oh, yes,' Janine sighed. 'And if it was just that I wouldn't mind. But I can't help thinking about Varushka, Leonid's mother.'

'I thought she was dead.'

'She is. She died six months ago, and he made a dash to Russia to be there at her bedside to say goodbye.'

'But doesn't he still have some business interests over there? He was probably visiting anyway.'

'No. We were planning a few days away, to celebrate my birthday, but he suddenly announced that he had to go to Russia urgently. He dashed off the same day and was gone nearly a week. He said it was business, but the day after he got back there was an e-mail from Leonid, thanking him for being there to say goodbye to Varushka. Of course I wasn't supposed to see it, and he doesn't

know that I did. But he's never mentioned her—
just told me a pack of lies.'

'But, Mum, it doesn't mean that he loved her.
It was probably for Leonid's sake.'

'Yes, his sons are more important to him than
anyone else,' Janine agreed wryly. 'More important than wives.'

'Did he ever make it up to you for your birthday?'

'He would claim that he did. I got a diamond
necklace, but we didn't go away. Taking a trip
involves time and work, but necklaces are easy.'
She added ironically, 'As I have reason to know.'

'Hathor,' Freya said, remembering that night
in Edfu.

'Yes, it makes you wonder if that's how Horus
bought her off.' She gave a wry smile. 'I'm sure
Hathor always said the right thing to keep him
happy. That's what one learns to do.'

'I'm not so sure. Some of us never learn to do
that.'

'You'll learn with Jackson.'

'Will I? I don't think so. I guess I'm too clumsy.'

'You just need practice. It's lucky he'll be there in Russia.'

'Yes,' Freya murmured. 'He will, won't he?'

CHAPTER TWELVE

LEONID HANDLED ALL the arrangements for their trip to Russia. First they would go to the little town of Rostov, for the christening. Then they would spend a few days in Moscow, celebrating.

The flight for Russia left from Nice Airport. Amos, Janine and Freya began the journey by staying overnight in Nice, where they were joined by Cassie and Marcel.

'Since the baby was born in Moscow, why isn't it being christened there?' Marcel wanted to know as they all shared a drink in the evening.

'Rostov was his mother's home,' Cassie said. 'He just managed to tell her about the baby before she died, and he wants to christen it in the church where she's buried.'

'Fancy Leonid being sentimental!' Marcel exclaimed.

'Hush,' Freya urged quietly. 'Don't let my mother hear you.'

'Surely she's not troubled by Varushka?' Marcel said. 'Not after all the other women our father's had?'

It was Cassie who silenced him with a finger over her lips. She drew him away with an understanding smile for Freya, who mouthed *Thank you*.

She was relieved to see that Janine was contentedly drinking coffee. She wasn't pleased about going to Rostov, but she hadn't said so to Amos. To Freya's eyes she had seemed to settle into calm resignation.

Jackson wasn't there. He was coming from London and would arrive after everyone else. She wondered how they would meet. Would he try to avoid her? Could she blame him if he did?

Next day they travelled to Rostov, where Leonid and Perdita were waiting to welcome them with open arms. That evening there was a merry party in the hotel.

Except for Jackson, everyone was now there. The Falcon brothers missed no chance to get together as a family, and this was the first occasion since Freya's aborted wedding. She recalled Jackson once saying that he felt especially close to Darius, the eldest. Of Amos's five sons they were the only two who shared a mother as well as a father.

She liked Darius, and had been enchanted by Harriet, the wife he'd met on Herringdean, the island that had become his in payment of a debt. Everyone had expected him to sell up as soon as possible and return to his life as a business magnate. But with Harriet's help he'd become enchanted by island life and now he was settled there for ever, with her and the child she had borne him.

Harriet saw her first and waved. Freya waved back and rushed to join her.

Both Harriet and Darius regarded Freya sympathetically.

'How's life treating you since the wedding?' Harriet asked gently.

'Everything's fine,' Freya said cheerfully.

'Isn't Amos making your life a misery, trying to tie you to Jackson? He's the only son left.'

'No chance. Jackson and I would never suit each other. We're both too set in our ways.'

'Set in your ways?' Marcel echoed. 'Him? You?'

'Jackson doesn't like being said no to. And I'm

an awkward customer who likes saying no. Just think how miserable I'd make him.'

'You mean you think he's too like Amos?' Harriet ventured.

'I've heard people say that.'

'I know he's inherited Amos's forcefulness,' Harriet agreed. 'But there's a side of him that he doesn't show too often. He's drawn to people who need his protection.'

Freya nodded. She had reason to know that.

'And not just people,' Harriet added.

'I don't understand.'

'At one time he used to do nature documentaries. I remember him coming to Herringdean to shoot a programme about our wildlife, and there was a baby seal who'd got stranded in an awkward place. Jackson became his guardian and protector. He said the seal's mother would be looking for him, and he must be taken care of until she arrived. He settled down beside him and stayed there for two days and nights, waiting for the mother to come searching for her baby. He said he wasn't going to let her find a dead body.

'He refused to move away, even to eat. Darius and I used to take food to him, otherwise he'd have starved. And he wouldn't let anyone film them in case the baby was upset, so we had to keep the crew away as well. I remember we stayed with him one night, and he was so gentle and loving with that little creature. In the end the mother arrived and Jackson carried her baby to her.

'The boss was furious that he wouldn't let the cameras get near him. Everyone thought Jackson would seize the wonderful publicity it would give him. But all he cared about was that helpless little creature. When it was all over the boss fired him and he had to find another job. That's how he came to be working for Dan.'

'He never told me,' Freya breathed.

'He doesn't talk about that side of himself. I think he's afraid it will make him sound like a softie.'

'What's wrong with being a softie?' Freya demanded with a touch of indignation.

'Nothing. I agree. I think he's always been a bit embarrassed about having a sweet nature in case it makes Amos ashamed of him. But you could say that it's another aspect of being a bully.'

'What?'

'The instinct to take command and override any opposition. A nasty bully says, "I'm taking charge and you'll do what I say. No argument." A nice bully says, "I'm taking charge and I'm going to protect you, whatever you say, and woe betide anyone who tries to stop me. Even you."'

'Yes,' Freya murmured. 'Oh, yes….'

A scene was playing out in her memory. Suddenly she was back in the time when she'd first discovered why Dan had fled and Jackson had concealed the worst facts from her. She'd flown at him in fury and he'd tried to defend himself, pleading, 'You're saying I was wrong to try protect you from more pain? I failed, but I still think I was right to try.'

'You're so sure you know best,' she'd raged.

'That's why people do things. Because they think it's right.'

He'd taken the blame for Dan's behaviour as few men would have done. She'd attacked him, despised him, frozen him out, and he'd endured it all as the price of protecting her. When she'd relented just a little he'd offered her his love.

Was this man a bully?

Or a guardian angel?

Or both?

Another memory returned: Larry telling her about the fight Jackson had had with a production company. He'd won, but at the cost of his job, which was how he'd come to work for Dan. Nobody knew the details, but it was spoken of as proof of Jackson's toughness, his determination to impose his own will.

'But it was this,' she murmured. 'Protecting a baby seal. Who would believe it? Except me. I'd believe it, because he protected *me*.'

She'd accused him of being driven only by guilt, and he'd never denied that he was troubled about the part he'd played. But there was more. He was a man who reached out to creatures in pain because he yearned to be needed. And perhaps some of that need was rooted in the unhappy childhood about which he'd confided in her and no one else.

She had struggled to understand him and thought she'd succeeded. But she had failed. If she'd seen as deeply into his heart as she now did she would have drawn closer, perhaps close enough to be the woman he longed for and needed.

She slipped away as soon as possible. Now she needed to be alone—to think about the way the world had changed yet again.

Once in her room she paced back and forth, tormented by the knowledge that what she wanted most in life was slipping away from her—and it was her own doing. Would she ever see Jackson again?

There was a knock on her door. Reluctantly she opened it, ready to drive away whoever dared to intrude on her sadness. Then she gasped.

Stunned, she stared at Jackson, trying to believe what she was seeing. His face was tense, almost haggard. Where was the confident Jackson? Who was this man with an air of hesitancy, almost defeat?

She had a feeling that at an unfriendly word from her he would turn tail and run, and she knew an impulse to reach out and say kindly, *It's all right. I'll take care of everything.*

Instead she said simply, 'Come in.'

He hesitated, and she guessed the memory of their last meeting was still vivid in his mind. She took his hand and drew him into her room.

'Thank you,' he said. 'I won't trouble you long.

There are things I must say, and then I'll go and not bother you again. But I beg you to hear me out first.'

'You don't have to beg me.'

He answered not in words but with a wry smile that reminded her of all that had happened between them.

'You don't,' she repeated. 'What can I do for you, Jackson?'

'I've come to do something for you—something I hope will make you glad.' He drew a long breath. 'Dan has been in touch with me.'

She waited for the leap of her heart that this news would once have given her. But nothing happened.

'He wants me to do a few programmes for him,' Jackson continued.

'But surely you're under contract to Larry's firm?'

'Partly, but I can still do some freelance projects. I've had a couple of meetings with Dan, but they weren't very productive about work. All he can talk about is you.'

'Tell him not to worry. I'm not coming after him with a shotgun.'

'He's not worried about that. He's more concerned about coming after you with a wedding ring.'

'That's a very bad joke.'

'It's not a joke. He keeps bringing the conversation around to you. He's realised what a big mistake he's made.'

Freya stepped back and regarded him, trying to read his face. But it was unreadable. Inside herself the reaction to Dan's name was the same as before. Nothing.

'I think that's really why he's been in touch with me,' Jackson continued. 'He wants me to talk to you on his behalf.'

'Then he's got a hell of a nerve!' she said indignantly.

'Has he? I wonder…'

'This makes no sense. If Dan wants to talk to me, why doesn't he just call me?'

'He's afraid to. He thinks you'll slam the phone down on him.'

'Which I would.'

'I don't think so. Not at first anyway. You'd hang on a few minutes for the pleasure of hearing him crawl.'

'Oh, yes, I'm known for my spite and vindictiveness.'

'No, just for your ability to stand up to a man and refuse to take any nonsense. I know all about that from my own experience. But Dan doesn't want to put a foot wrong.'

'Why not? He's put everything else wrong.'

'Yes, I told him that. He understands that he must do this the right way, and I promised to talk to you.'

'Then you're mad. I'm not in love with Dan—if I ever was. That's over—finished. I've told you this before.'

'Yes, you've told me this before—again and again. Maybe too often, as if you were trying to convince yourself.'

'Perhaps in the beginning, but not now.'

That had only been her way of coping. At last she understood the difference between the shallow feelings Dan had inspired and the passionate love that had grown in her for Jackson.

'Freya, listen to me. I've been thinking long and hard about why I never stood a chance of winning your love. And at last I know. I'd always suspected it, but I wouldn't let myself face it because I couldn't bear to. The fact is that you've never stopped loving Dan.'

'Please—'

'And he loves you. You can put the past right. Let me go back and tell him he has a chance.'

'I don't know how you can bring yourself to talk like this,' she said in a fury. '*This* is all your protestations of love for me meant? How dare you?'

At once his temper rose in response to hers.

'You stupid woman!' he snapped. 'Don't you understand that I'm doing this because I *do* love you?'

'Handing me over to another man?

'A man you love as you could never love me. A man who can give you all the happiness that I can't. I want you to have that happiness more than I've ever wanted anything in the world.'

The words were tender but his voice was harsh: the voice of a man determined to do things his way—even if he broke his own heart in the process.

Freya tried to speak, but now the tears were coming fast enough to choke her.

'Perhaps I really am stupid,' she said huskily. 'But I can't get my mind around this.'

His anger died. 'It's not your mind that needs to understand,' he said quietly.

'But my heart tells me that this is madness. Even if I believed in Dan's love, that doesn't change the kind of unreliable man he is.'

'Your love can improve him, make him want to be better.'

'And if it doesn't?'

'Then I'll always help you in any way you want. I can go back to work for Dan, and if necessary I can knock some sense into him. And if you need someone to turn to I'll always be there.'

She stared at him, stunned by the implications of what he was suggesting.

'But you can't do that,' she whispered. 'It would spoil your career, swallow up your life, leave you with nothing.'

'I have nothing now,' he said simply. 'As for my life—it's yours. You can't send me away because I won't go as long as there's even a hint that you might need me. And if I can believe that you *don't* need me, I'll just wait until it happens again.'

She couldn't believe what she was hearing. Jackson, a determined, forceful man, was putting himself at her mercy. Now the mask was tossed aside, the armour removed. What was left was the real man—vulnerable, defenceless, unprotected, and above all content for her to know it.

'Do you understand?' he asked. 'I belong to you and you can't get rid of me.' He gave a faint smile. 'You see what a bully I am.'

'Yes, the worst kind,' she murmured, moving closer to him. 'The kind who thinks he knows what's best for someone else. You won't listen when I tell you I don't love Dan. But I don't—and I'm going to force you to accept that, because I can be a bully too.'

A new look had come into his face. Confusion, mixed with hope and a little alarm, as though he feared to hope for too much.

She met his gaze, silently telling him what to believe.

'My methods are ruthless,' she said, 'and by the time I'm finished you'll have to believe me.'

'How are you going to manage that?' he whispered.

'Like this.'

Reaching up, she drew his head down far enough to rest her lips against his.

'Freya—'

'Kiss me, Jackson. That's an order. You're not the only one who likes to be obeyed. Kiss me.'

He obeyed with fervour, wrapping his arms right round her so that she couldn't have escaped if she'd wanted to. But she didn't want to. She wanted the pressure of his lips, growing fiercer with every moment. She wanted the feel of him shaking with desire against her own body, which was also shaking as never before—not for Dan, not for any other man, only for this man in her arms, where she was determined to keep him.

She had everything she wanted. He was hers as completely as she was his. His lips told her so, as did his arms, and the powerful beat of his heart that she could just hear. She wanted him with an intensity that only one thing could satisfy, and she was determined to have it.

When she drew him towards the bed he hesitated for a tiny moment, as though not daring to believe that his dreams could come true. But then doubt was swept away by desire and they fell onto the bed together, kissing, embracing, murmuring, pulling at each other's clothes until there was not a stitch left between them.

He made love to her with a mixture of tenderness and passion that left her dizzy. She responded with everything in her, and had the delight of seeing in his eyes that she had taken him by surprise.

Afterwards he held her close, her head against his chest, so that she could hear his heart again, beating more slowly now, with sweet, gentle contentment.

'I feel as though we've only just met,' he murmured.

'Yes, that's just how it is,' she said happily. 'This is a new life for us. And there's something else as well. Thanks to Harriet, I know you better than ever before.'

'Harriet?'

'She told me about that baby seal on Herringdean, and the sacrifices you made to protect it. I'd already heard a rumour about how you quarrelled with a production firm and stormed out, but it made you sound grim and threatening.'

'Good,' he said at once. 'If my father knew the truth he'd cut me out of his life.'

'But it made me want you in my life. I began to understand how much you need me and how deeply you long to be needed in return. Not just loved, but needed.'

'Yes,' he breathed. 'Yes. I didn't realise before. Freya, is this really happening to us?'

'I don't know. I can hardly believe it. It's so beautiful. Can it be true?'

'It can be as true as we make it.'

'Yes,' she murmured. 'Oh, yes.'

'There are still questions whirling in my brain,' he murmured against her hair. 'You were so much against me. You didn't want my love. At least, you said you didn't. When I held you in my arms and kissed you I dared to hope that you wanted me a little—'

'More than a little, my darling. I've wanted you for quite a while, but I wouldn't admit it even to myself. I was afraid. After what happened with Dan I didn't want to fall in love—'

'Especially with me,' he said wryly.

'Yes. I was more afraid of getting close to you than anyone else—maybe because I knew it was inevitable. That night in Monte Carlo I resisted you because I felt caught up in something beyond my control. I know now that I was right, but I shouldn't have been afraid of it because the fate beyond my control was love.'

'Mine too. That's why I came here as Dan's spokesman. I thought it would be what you wanted.'

'You thought I'd let you spend your life watching over me?'

'*Let* me?' His voice became teasing. 'You couldn't stop me.'

'Oh, yes, I could. There's a very simple way.'

'Tell me.'

'I won't marry Dan. I'm going to marry you. That way *I'll* be *your* protector. So come on— we're getting married. That's an order.'

'Hey, I was going to say that.'

'Tough. I got in first.'

'Yes,' he said happily. 'You did. I guess I'll have to get used to you taking command.'

'You'll have to get used to me protecting you as much as you protect me.'

'Joint partnership.'

'Fifty-fifty.'

Solemnly they shook hands.

'I can hardly believe in such happiness.' She

sighed blissfully. 'And it's even more lovely in this place, where so many of the family are happy too. All except—' She broke off and sighed.

'Your mother and my father,' Jackson supplied. 'Yes, it's sad, isn't it? How can we really enjoy our own happiness when things are still so wrong between them? At first I thought they'd sort it out soon and rediscover what they used to have. But it's getting worse.'

'It's because he overheard Mum say she had doubts about him and wasn't sure that they'd stay together,' Freya recalled. 'That really seemed to knock him sideways.'

'Yes, he's used to women wanting him more than he wants them. I'm sure he could win her over if he tried, but he doesn't know how to give in, to say he's sorry.'

'He'd see it as a weakness,' Freya said. 'And he avoids that like the plague. I remember him telling you that you shouldn't let anyone know anything about you that they could see as weak and use against you.'

'Right. He's never understood that when you really love someone you're not afraid to let them know your weakness, the way you know mine.'

'Mum hated coming here to Russia. She thinks Varushka was the great love of Amos's life because of the way he rushed out here to her deathbed.'

'She's wrong. I think Janine means more to him than any other woman has, but he doesn't know how to show it. Even with her he can't risk seeming vulnerable, and it could be the worst mistake he's ever made.'

'But if they can make it right,' Freya said hesitantly, 'how will you feel? After what you told me about your mother—'

'I know. But I like Janine. She's always been pleasant to me. And she's his victim too. As for Amos, he's still my father, and I'd still like to see him find happiness in love.' He drew her closer. 'Especially now that I've found it myself.'

'Yes,' she murmured. 'Enough about them. I want to think only of you. Come to me, my darling—come to me—that's right—yes—*yes*—'

The christening was held in a little church on the edge of town. Everything went perfectly. Janine showed no sign of trouble, and Freya began to hope that all would be well.

Afterwards Leonid led the way to his mother's grave at the back, followed by the family, including Amos and Janine.

Freya tried to draw her mother away, but Janine resisted.

'I will go where my husband goes,' she said.

Varushka's marble gravestone was simple but lovely. Flowers lay around the base, put there earlier by Leonid.

'It's beautiful,' Charlene said. 'I wish I could read the Russian words.'

'They just give the date she was born and the date she died,' Leonid told her.

He said the words in English, and at once Freya sensed disaster. For the date of Varushka's death was the exact date of Janine's birthday.

She had coped with Amos's absence on that day, but now the coincidence of the dates seemed to make everything worse. Janine didn't speak, but she turned and walked away.

Freya hurried after her.

'Mum, the date's just an unlucky coincidence.'

'I spent that day in tears. It was my birthday, and we were going to have a lovely celebration holiday together. But that was the day he said goodbye to *her*—held her in his arms, kissed her, told her he loved her. The very same day.'

'He's coming over,' Freya murmured.

Amos and Jackson were approaching.

Janine turned to face Amos, who tensed.

'What's the matter?' he demanded. 'Why do you look at me like that? I was only paying my respects.'

'Drop the pretence,' Janine snapped. '*She's* the one who has your heart. I've known for months now—ever since you dumped me to rush here to her deathbed. You chose her over me.'

'No!' Amos said explosively. 'No, that wasn't what happened. I came because I had to.'

'Yes, she wanted you, so you had to. When we get home I'm leaving you.'

Amos drew a sharp breath. Freya and Jackson exchanged glances, both sensing that Amos was about to make a momentous decision.

'All right,' he said. 'Here's the truth. I didn't come here from choice. I was blackmailed.'

'Oh, Amos, please—do you expect me to believe that Leonid blackmailed you?'

'No, not him. He knew nothing about it. It

was—' He stopped and a shudder went through him. 'It was Perdita.'

Janine didn't speak, but her face showed her scepticism.

Amos tore at his hair.

'It's true,' he cried. 'Perdita was a journalist in those days. She found out about a slightly iffy deal I'd done. She could have caused me a lot of trouble if she'd talked. And she threatened to do exactly that if I didn't come out here to see Varushka before she died. That was why it happened so suddenly. I only had a few hours to save myself from disaster. I didn't want to come. Over the years I'd seen Varushka so rarely that I barely knew her. But I had no choice.'

He took a deep, painful breath.

'That's the truth, my dear. Please believe me.'

The word 'please' made everyone look up, alert, wondering if they'd heard properly. Amos had actually said *please* to a woman.

And Freya saw something else. There on Amos's face was the same defenceless look she'd seen on Jackson's face the previous night.

It was a look that neither man had ever worn before. She was sure of it. And it meant the same:

a willingness to sacrifice everything to win the valued prize.

Horus the Elder and Horus the Younger had achieved victory at the same time. She could almost hear the cries of triumph from the Edfu temple.

Janine's gaze was fixed on Amos, who was totally still, tense with apprehension as nobody had ever seen him before. Then she gave a cry of joy and threw herself into his arms. He seized her fiercely, burying his face against her neck and saying her name in a muffled voice. By now the rest of the family had caught up, and they gave a big cheer.

'He did it!' Jackson said triumphantly to Freya. 'He told her about his weakness. He trusted her with it. That's the bit that makes all the difference.'

'Oh, yes!' she exclaimed joyfully. 'She's the one.'

Amos lifted his head. His cheeks were wet.

'I guess I still have to catch up with a few things,' he said huskily.

'Just a few,' Jackson agreed.

'And to prove to you that I've seen the light

I promise to leave you two alone. I won't try to make you marry each other. That's over, for good.'

'It was over anyway,' Jackson told him. 'We got engaged this morning.'

More cheering.

The whole family rioted in delight, dancing around them, slapping them on the back.

Jackson and Freya were barely aware of them. Looking into each other's eyes, they saw only what mattered to them, what would matter for the rest of their lives.

'Let's go away,' Jackson said. 'I have a lot of things to say to you.'

'And I to you. But they don't really need saying.'

'No, but I want to say them anyway.'

They drifted off. The ground sloped gently upwards, so that after a while they could look back on where the family was still rejoicing, waving up to them. They laughed as they saw Amos give them a victory gesture.

'I guess he's got what he always wanted,' Freya said.

'Yes. Look, he's trying to placate Janine in case

she makes him suffer. I guess that's how it'll always be between them from now on. Between us too, perhaps.'

'Don't worry. I won't be too hard on you,' she teased.

'Is that a promise?'

'Wait and find out.'

They shared a gentle kiss, stood for a moment contentedly resting against each other. Then they resumed their walk, leaving the others far behind—leaving the whole world behind. For they had a new world now, one in which nothing and nobody else existed.

And that was how it would always be.

EPILOGUE

THEIR WEDDING WAS a quiet affair in a church so small and so deep in the country that birdsong could be heard during the service. This was Freya's choice, and Amos had acceded to it willingly. All he'd asked was to be the man who gave her away to his son, and she'd happily agreed.

She had no fear that her groom would go missing this time. She knew that no power on earth could take Jackson from her. He'd told her so in words and actions, and she knew it on a level too deep for words.

All the Falcons were present. Nothing could have kept them away from this wedding. They smiled as Amos and Freya moved slowly down the aisle, noting how Jackson kept his eyes fixed on his bride, as though only half daring to believe that she was really there. They all enjoyed the moment when Amos handed Freya to her groom and couldn't resist giving a thumbs-up sign to celebrate his triumph.

Then he slipped away to join Janine in a pew. Together they listened as the priest began to speak the words that would unite the family as never before.

'We are gathered here to join together this man and this woman…'

This man and this woman.

Out of sight, Amos took hold of his wife's hand, squeezed it a little, and sighed with relief when she squeezed back. Since that day in Russia when they had rediscovered each other he'd had the sense of living in a new universe, one that had yet to be explored.

The wedding service continued, with the bride and groom taking it in turn to utter their vows.

For better, for worse.

Amos murmured in Janine's ear, 'Try to forgive me for the worse.'

Smiling, she turned to meet his eyes, murmuring, 'From now on it's going to be better.'

At last it was time for the bride and groom to leave the church, ready to start their marriage. And there behind them were Amos and

Janine, also making a new start that only they understood.

Perhaps Jackson and Freya came closest to perceiving the truth.

As they lay in each other's arms that night she murmured, 'There was more than one bride and groom today.'

'Yes, I thought so too,' he said with a warm chuckle. 'When you think how nearly they missed each other—'

'How nearly *we* missed each other. If you hadn't come up with that mad performance—'

'It was true. Dan really had contacted me.'

'Yes, but the rest—the things you said about watching over me, forcing him to be a good husband. Surely you couldn't really have done that?'

In the dark warmth of the bed she felt him chuckle.

'Couldn't I? I don't know. I was desperate enough to try anything that might work.'

She thumped him lightly.

'You lousy, cheating so-and-so. You just said what you knew would get you your own way.'

'That's the best reason for saying anything. I

wanted you and I didn't care what I had to do to get you. After all, I'm a Falcon.'

'So am I now, so you'd better watch out. But you couldn't *really* have lived up to that stuff about being my guardian angel even if it meant sacrificing your career. Could you?'

'I hope so, but the honest answer is that I don't know myself well enough to predict how well I'd have succeeded. I still have a lot to learn about who I am and what I can do. But I can't learn it alone. You'll have to teach me.'

'Hmm. Now, that might be interesting.'

'More than interesting…'

He drew her closer, wrapping his arms about her with an intensity that was both commanding and protective.

'Why don't we start now?' he whispered.

* * * * *

Mills & Boon® Large Print
May 2014

THE DIMITRAKOS PROPOSITION
Lynne Graham

HIS TEMPORARY MISTRESS
Cathy Williams

A MAN WITHOUT MERCY
Miranda Lee

THE FLAW IN HIS DIAMOND
Susan Stephens

FORGED IN THE DESERT HEAT
Maisey Yates

THE TYCOON'S DELICIOUS DISTRACTION
Maggie Cox

A DEAL WITH BENEFITS
Susanna Carr

MR (NOT QUITE) PERFECT
Jessica Hart

ENGLISH GIRL IN NEW YORK
Scarlet Wilson

THE GREEK'S TINY MIRACLE
Rebecca Winters

THE FINAL FALCON SAYS I DO
Lucy Gordon

0414 Rom LP

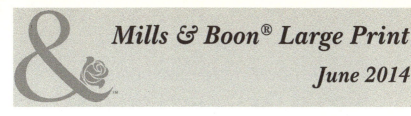

Mills & Boon® Large Print

June 2014

A BARGAIN WITH THE ENEMY
Carole Mortimer

A SECRET UNTIL NOW
Kim Lawrence

SHAMED IN THE SANDS
Sharon Kendrick

SEDUCTION NEVER LIES
Sara Craven

WHEN FALCONE'S WORLD STOPS TURNING
Abby Green

SECURING THE GREEK'S LEGACY
Julia James

AN EXQUISITE CHALLENGE
Jennifer Hayward

TROUBLE ON HER DOORSTEP
Nina Harrington

HEIRESS ON THE RUN
Sophie Pembroke

THE SUMMER THEY NEVER FORGOT
Kandy Shepherd

DARING TO TRUST THE BOSS
Susan Meier

Discover more romance at

www.millsandboon.co.uk

- ❤ WIN great prizes in our exclusive competitions

- ❤ BUY new titles before they hit the shops

- ❤ BROWSE new books and REVIEW your favourites

- ❤ SAVE on new books with the Mills & Boon® Bookclub™

- ❤ DISCOVER new authors

PLUS, to chat about your favourite reads, get the latest news and find special offers:

- Find us on facebook.com/millsandboon
- Follow us on twitter.com/millsandboonuk
- ❤ Sign up to our newsletter at millsandboon.co.uk

Hymns (Liturgical)

THE HUNDRED BEST
LATIN HYMNS